This book belongs to

Maura

roxie and the

hooligans at buzzard's roost

PHYLLIS REYNOLDS NAYLOR

with illustrations by ALEXANDRA BOIGER

A Caitlyn Dlouhy Book

ATHENEUM BOOKS FOR YOUNG READERS

NEW YORK LONDON TORONTO SYDNEY NEW DELHI

𝒜
atheneum

ATHENEUM BOOKS FOR YOUNG READERS
An imprint of Simon & Schuster Children's Publishing Division
1230 Avenue of the Americas, New York, New York 10020
This book is a work of fiction. Any references to historical events, real people, or real places are used fictitiously. Other names, characters, places, and events are products of the author's imagination, and any resemblance to actual events or places or persons, living or dead, is entirely coincidental.
Text copyright © 2018 by Phyllis Reynolds Naylor
Illustrations copyright © 2018 by Alexandra Boiger
All rights reserved, including the right of reproduction in whole or in part in any form.
ATHENEUM BOOKS FOR YOUNG READERS is a registered trademark
of Simon & Schuster, Inc. Atheneum logo is a trademark of Simon & Schuster, Inc.
For information about special discounts for bulk purchases, please contact
Simon & Schuster Special Sales at 1-866-506-1949 or business@simonandschuster.com.
The Simon & Schuster Speakers Bureau can bring authors to your live event.
For more information or to book an event, contact the Simon & Schuster Speakers Bureau at 1-866-248-3049 or visit our website at www.simonspeakers.com.
Also available in an Atheneum Books for Young Readers hardcover edition
Book design by Ann Bobco
The text for this book was set in Augustal.
The illustrations for this book were rendered in pencil on paper, scanned, and edited in Photoshop.
Manufactured in the United States of America
0419 OFF
First Atheneum Books for Young Readers paperback edition May 2019
10 9 8 7 6 5 4 3 2 1
The Library of Congress has cataloged the hardcover edition as follows:
Names: Naylor, Phyllis Reynolds, author. | Boiger, Alexandra, illustrator.
Title: Roxie and the hooligans at Buzzard's Roost / Phyllis Reynolds Naylor ; illustrated by Alexandra Boiger.
Description: First edition. | New York : Atheneum, [2017] | "A Caitlyn Dlouhy Book." | Summary: The hooligans sneak along when Roxie Warbler goes on a beach vacation with her beloved Uncle Dangerfoot, and soon they uncover the secret invention he has been hiding from his nemesis, Alfred Applejack.
Identifiers: LCCN 2017005302 | ISBN 9781481437820 (hc)
ISBN 9781481437837 (pbk) | ISBN 9781481437844 (eBook)
Subjects: | CYAC: Adventure and adventurers—Fiction. | Inventions—Fiction. | Behavior—Fiction. | Beaches—Fiction. | Resourcefulness—Fiction.
Classification: LCC PZ7.N24 Rox 2018 | DDC [Fic]—dc23
LC record available at https://lccn.loc.gov/2017005302

contents

roxie

and the hooligans at
buzzard's roost

· ON THE ROAD ·

After Roxie became friends with the hooligans, they were still a troublesome lot.

Helvetia Hagus, the sturdy girl with knee socks rolled down to her ankles, would often bump another child out of line, just so she could stand next to Roxie at lunchtime.

Simon Surly would punch the nose of any boy in Public School Number Thirty-Seven who dared make fun of Roxie's big ears.

Freddy Filch would swipe a toffee candy from a classmate just to slip it into Roxie's pocket at recess.

And wiry little Smoky Jo would follow Roxie around like a shadow, telling everyone, in her squeaky voice, that she and Roxie Warbler were a team.

Because everyone along this little stretch of New England shoreline, from the town of Hasty Pudding to Hamburger-on-Bun, and even those in the village of Swiss-on-Rye, knew the story by heart: how Roxie and the hooligans had outsmarted the bank robbers, making their small village of Chin-in-Hand proud!

None of that would have happened, however, if the hooligans hadn't been perfectly dreadful to

Roxie because of her large ears, and to Norman, her best friend, just because he wore glasses. They had teased and tormented and tripped and trapped them so often that Roxie had gone to Public School Number Thirty-Seven each morning with an ache in the pit of her stomach.

And then . . . the awful day that the hooligans had chased her into a dumpster, all piling in after her, and a truck had arrived to cart it off to a barge, which was emptied far out at sea. Somehow the children had managed to swim to an island where two bank robbers were hiding. . . .

If it hadn't been for Norman back on the playground, who, even though the hooligans had knocked his glasses off, had figured out what was happening with the dumpster, there might never

3

have been the dramatic rescue by helicopter that was talked about for many weeks.

Roxie, however, was a bit tired of all the attention, and was delighted when school was out for the summer, because Uncle Dangerfoot was taking her on vacation to a place called Buzzard's Roost to celebrate her daring adventure.

"I wish you and Daddy were coming too," Roxie said as her mother brushed her hair. Roxie's ears stuck straight out from her head like the handles on a sugar bowl, so her hair was often a tangle.

"I do too, Love, but Papa and I have to tend the shop," her mother said. "You'll come back and tell us all about it. And don't forget to take your bathing suit and sandals."

Right that very minute, Uncle Dangerfoot

4

drove up to the cottage in a car that pulled a small trailer. A beach umbrella stuck out one window of the trailer, and a kite bobbed from the other. Across the street, the hooligans watched, their mouths turned down at the corners.

Mrs. Warbler had tea and crumpets ready for him when Uncle Dangerfoot came up the walk. The man who had wrestled alligators and jumped from planes was not to be kept waiting, and he never began a trip without a good, bracing cup of hot tea.

He wore a jungle helmet and a tan safari jacket with brass buttons. And, as always, he carried a long slender cane, which could, in an instant, become a harpoon, a gun, an umbrella, or a walking stick, depending on the circumstances and the weather.

Nine-year-old Roxie always looked forward to his visits, for he had traveled all over the world with Lord Thistlebottom from London. And Lord Thistlebottom was the famous author of the book *Lord Thistlebottom's Book of Pitfalls and How to Survive Them.*

"Come in! Come in!" said Roxie's father, shaking the uncle's hand and ushering him to the big easy chair with a footstool at the ready.

This time, however, instead of telling the family about his latest adventure, Uncle Dangerfoot asked, "How are you getting along with that hooligan bunch now, Roxie?"

"Well," she replied, "Helvetia doesn't try to tape my ears back anymore."

Mrs. Warbler folded her hands in her lap and smiled. "Because Roxie was the only one who

6

could hear those robbers creeping through the forest, so what would they have done without her?"

"And Simon doesn't throw things at me anymore," said Roxie.

Her father was smiling proudly too. "Because Roxie showed them how to dig a trench and hide in it at night when those robbers came looking for them," he told Uncle Dangerfoot.

"Freddy Filch doesn't hit me anymore," said Roxie.

Mrs. Warbler made a clicking sound with her tongue. "And shameful that he ever did!" she declared. "But he'll not be hitting you again, after you were the one to slip into those robbers' tent and get food and water for the others."

"And Smoky Jo follows me wherever I go, just in case I need her," said Roxie.

"Thinks the world of our Roxie, ever since she saw her eat a bug," said Mr. Warbler with a chuckle. "Mean and sassy as those kids can be, not a one was brave enough to eat an insect if they had to."

"It was a grub," Roxie explained. "Wrapped in a dandelion leaf."

"Aha! Survival food! Page 243 of Lord Thistlebottom's book!" cried her uncle. "Jolly good!"

"So we get along," Roxie explained. "Sometimes I wish they wouldn't hang around so much, but it's better being friends than enemies."

"Absolutely," said her uncle. "And speaking of friends, I promised that you could invite a friend. Have you decided who that will be?"

"Norman!" Roxie told him. "He's been my best friend forever, and he's packed and waiting."

"Then we shall drink our tea and be off before it gets much later," said her uncle. When he had finished his crumpet, he turned to Roxie's mother: "I've hired a housekeeper for the week to watch over the children, dear sister; she'll look after Roxie's every need."

"You are so kind," Mrs. Warbler told him.

So Roxie said good-bye to her parents and carried her small suitcase to the car. The hooligans were gone now, but three blocks away, Uncle Dangerfoot stopped at the little house where Norman was waiting with his backpack. He was a chubby boy with thick glasses, who the hooligans used to tease and torment just as they had bullied Roxie.

Norman said good afternoon to Uncle Dangerfoot, tossed his backpack into the car, and climbed in beside Roxie. And soon they were on their way.

It was almost five hours later, and evening, when they reached a large old house that sat back a bit from the ocean, surrounded by scraggly trees and sea grass.

Roxie's big ears caught the sound of waves breaking onshore. She rolled down the window to smell the sea air. Though her little village of Chin-in-Hand was also not far from the ocean, it had no beach, no sand, no place for children to wade or swim; the water was cold, and there

10

were certainly no beach houses like this one.

Actually, she and Norman had fallen asleep on the long drive to Buzzard's Roost and on to Windswept House where they would be staying. They were a bit groggy and very stiff.

"The Widow Bitterworth lives here with her infant son," Uncle Dangerfoot said, "and I'm sure the housekeeper will have a good supper for us."

"I'd just like to stretch my legs!" Roxie said, climbing out and dragging her suitcase from the car.

"I'd like to go barefoot," Norman declared.

"Plenty of time for that," Uncle Dangerfoot said.

"Why do they call it Buzzard's Roost?" Roxie asked, looking around.

"Do you see that line of dead trees along the road?" her uncle said. "Buzzards seem to gather there, I'm told. Always have. Now, let me get my trunk from the trailer and we'll go inside."

The breeze tossed Roxie's hair up, down, and around. It was exciting to visit somewhere far from Chin-in-Hand, where times were hard and people did not get to travel much. She felt lucky to have a somewhat-famous uncle to take her places.

Uncle Dangerfoot reached for the latch on the trailer and opened the door.

"What in thunder . . . ?" he bellowed.

Roxie stared as Helvetia Hagus, Simon Surly, Freddy Filch, and Smoky Jo came tumbling out.

•THE WIDOW BITTERWORTH•

The hooligans looked hot and sweaty and mean.

"About time you unlatched that door!" Helvetia complained. "The moron who built that trailer forgot to put a handle on the inside."

"We almost smothered to death," added Simon.

"I was squashed the whole time between a

rubber raft and a deck chair," said Freddy.

"What is the meaning of this?" Uncle Dangerfoot sputtered. "How dare you invite yourselves along?"

"Well, you never bothered to invite us, so what else could we do?" said Helvetia, wiping one arm across her damp forehead. "Nobody ever asks us to go anywhere."

"But, how did you lock yourselves in?" asked Roxie.

"I latched the door for 'em and climbed in a window," bragged Smoky Jo. "So where's the beach?"

But Freddy was already scrambling to the top of a sand dune. "I see it! I see it!" he shouted, and he disappeared down the other side as the rest of the hooligans followed, braying like donkeys.

"Stop!" cried Uncle Dangerfoot, but his voice was lost to the sky, and only a gull soaring above bothered to answer.

With Roxie on one side and Norman on the other, Uncle Dangerfoot climbed the sand dune, puffing a little as he neared the top. On the beach below, the hooligans were racing toward the water, and as each wave broke on the shore, they screeched and bellowed, jumping backward and then lunging at the ocean again.

Roxie was sure that her uncle, with his cane, would go after them. But instead he pulled out his pocket watch, which could—Roxie knew— become a compass, a signal light, or a drinking cup, depending on the situation.

For now, it seemed, it was just a watch, because Uncle Dangerfoot checked the time,

16

looked at the hooligans, and then at his watch again.

"It is useless, I see, to contain the creatures just yet," he said. "They are hot and so are you, so why don't the two of you go join them, as I'm sure they will all be back again in about . . . uh . . . twenty minutes."

How did he figure that? Roxie wondered, but the ocean looked inviting to her as well, so she and Norman took off their shoes and socks and went rolling and tumbling down the dune.

The six of them danced in and out of the surf, the waves soaking the hems of their pants. They pulled up seaweed and tossed it high in the air. They searched for shells along the waterline and let the breeze cool their faces. Roxie wondered if the hooligans were remembering the last time

18

they were on a beach together—there on an island, building a distress marker in the sand out of rocks, afraid that the robbers would see them.

Up on the sand dune, the man who had wrestled alligators and jumped from planes was standing with his arms crossed, still holding his watch. And it wasn't long before Helvetia said, "I've got to have a drink of water."

"Me too," said Simon. "Ocean water's too salty."

"My throat's dry as an old sock," said Freddy.

"I wouldn't mind a hamburger, too," said Smoky Jo. But before she left, she traced her name in the wet sand with one finger.

So they all turned, picked up their shoes, and climbed back up the sand dune where Uncle Dangerfoot was waiting.

19

"When I say stop, you are to obey," he told the hooligans. "I could have paddled you, you know."

"We get enough of that without doing anything," Freddy told him.

They followed Uncle Dangerfoot along the dunes and down the other side. In the doorway of the big old house stood a round, apple-cheeked woman with a spoon in her hand.

"I think that's the housekeeper and cook," Roxie told Norman.

"Mrs. Tumbledry!" her uncle called. "What do you think we should do with all these children?"

"Feed them, I suppose," the woman replied. "Can't expect them to be good on an empty stomach." And, studying Simon, who was skinny

20

as a rail, she said, "That boy there would have to stand up twice to cast a shadow. Looks like he could use some dinner."

Uncle Dangerfoot sighed. "Get inside while I phone each of your parents to come get you," he told the hooligans, shooing them in with his cane.

"You can call all you want, but I'm betting not one of our dads will come for us," said Simon as they trooped through the door.

The old house had high ceilings, velvet draperies at the windows, and flowered rugs underfoot. The hooligans threw their shoes in a heap and eagerly drank the water Mrs. Tumbledry poured for them from a frosty pitcher.

As Uncle Dangerfoot called each of their parents, the hooligans ran from room to room, opening cupboards and pulling out drawers. They found rubber bands and began shooting them at one another. They opened a package of balloons, blew some up, then let them spin and zoom around. They made necklaces of paper clips and bounced Ping-Pong balls, and just as Simon had said, none of the parents were eager to have their children back anytime soon.

"Keep 'em for the week, would you, mister? 'Twould be a relief not to have 'em about," they said.

With that, Uncle Dangerfoot stood up straight as a lamppost. "Attention!" he cried, and tapped his cane hard on the floor. Instantly it transformed itself into a harpoon.

The hooligans sat up in astonishment. So did Norman, but Roxie had seen it before.

Uncle Dangerfoot tapped his cane twice, and it turned into a rifle. When he tapped it the third time, the hooligans ducked, but it became an umbrella. And when he gave it a final, sharp tap, it became a walking stick once again.

"I will have to decide what to do with you," he told the hooligans. "In the meantime, our house-keeper, Mrs. Tumbledry, has prepared dinner for us all. You will wash your hands in the kitchen, then seat yourselves at the dining-room table, where you will, I presume, conduct yourselves like ladies and gentlemen."

"Never been a lady before, and I'm not starting now," Helvetia muttered, but only loud enough for Roxie to hear, and the hooligans, joking and jostling, spilled into the kitchen. Roxie wondered if they had forgotten so soon that it was Uncle Dangerfoot, after all, who was in the helicopter that had rescued them from the island. Could they not act a little grateful?

At the sink, however, Freddy Filch pointed to Norman and said, "What's that creep doin' here, if we're not welcome?"

Instantly Roxie turned on him. "Norman is my friend, and as long as Uncle Dangerfoot lets you stay, you're going to be kind to him," she said.

At which point Helvetia Hagus rapped Freddy on the head and said, "And don't you forget it, neither!"

While the children got their plates from the cupboard, Mrs. Tumbledry added more peas to the stew and bread to the basket. Soon the large dining room was filled with the squeak of chairs,

24

the clink of forks, and an occasional "Pass the butter . . ." and finally, ". . . please."

Uncle Dangerfoot left the table early, and for a while Roxie wondered if he had gone away—driven into town, perhaps, and told the sheriff to come get the stowaways. You didn't just tell a housekeeper she would be making meals for three guests and show up with seven! Where would these extra children sleep, and who would wash their clothes?

Mrs. Tumbledry was a cheerful woman, however, and when all the stew and bread were gone, she asked who wanted pie. Six hands shot up in the air, and she told Norman he could come into the kitchen and put a scoop of ice cream on top of each piece.

When stomachs were full and the last drop of

milk had been drunk, there was the creak of stairs in the hall, the sound of footsteps, and suddenly Uncle Dangerfoot appeared in the doorway beside a tall figure dressed all in brown. Every child turned to look.

The woman was wearing a long brown dress that came up high on the neck. A brown veil covered her hair and face, and Roxie guessed that this was on account of recently losing her husband and becoming a widow. She even wore brown gloves.

"Children," Uncle Dangerfoot said, "I would like to present the Widow Bitterworth, who rents out rooms in this lovely house to support herself and her wee child. . . . Would you please say 'good evening' to Mrs. Bitterworth?"

"Good-eve-ning-Mis-sus-Bit-ter-worth," the

children chanted as if they were in school, though Roxie heard Freddy call her Mrs. "Bitter-wart" instead.

The tall woman stood very still. Slowly her head turned to the left. Slowly it turned to the right. Then silently, once again, she faced straight ahead, and somehow Roxie felt sure that the eyes behind the veil were looking directly at her.

• NOISES IN THE NIGHT •

Uncle Dangerfoot continued: "The Widow and I have come to a decision about your presence here at Windswept House. You may stay only as long as you obey the rules. This particular stretch of land is known as Buzzard's Roost. When you are outdoors, you may go north as far as the rocks; south as far as the inlet; west as far as the road; and east, of course, as far as the ocean. You are never to go in the water unless I or the Widow or Mrs. Tumbledry is with you. Is that understood?"

"Yes-Un-cle-Dan-ger-foot," the children chanted, and Roxie hoped they meant it.

"Also, each of you will have a special job to do. You'll find the lists in your bedrooms. Once you have done your work, you'll have the rest of the day to explore the dunes, play Frisbee on the sand, climb trees, and play croquet or any of the other games here in the hall closet."

Then the strange-looking lady in the long brown dress stepped forward. The veil was so thick that her eyes, nose, and mouth were hardly visible at all, though her chin was so large that the veil barely covered it. With her hands folded in front of her, she spoke in a low voice: "The boys will sleep in the blue room on second, the girls in the yellow. You will leave your dirty clothes outside your door every evening, and they will be washed the following morning. If you need extra clothing while you are here, which you surely will, you may search the drawers, where you will find various forgotten garments left by guests in the past."

A murmur went up among the hooligans.

"I'm not wearing anyone else's britches!" Helvetia declared, but Uncle Dangerfoot tapped the floor lightly with his cane, which brought immediate silence.

The Widow continued: "You are never to open a door without knocking first, and the third floor—where I live with my baby—is off limits. You will use the front staircase, as the back stairs are

30

for the housekeeper only, and Mrs. Tumbledry has the bedroom next to the girls', if there is an emergency during the night. Breakfast is at eight o'clock, lunch is served at noon, and dinner at six. Welcome to Windswept House, and I wish you a pleasant good night." With that, the Widow turned and went back upstairs.

"Will you be sleeping in the boys' room, Uncle Dangerfoot?" Roxie asked.

"No, my dear, I have a cot down here in the library, for I'll be doing a little work on this vacation. Just one of my many projects. And should anyone get the idea to sneak downstairs and start some mischief, I will be here to catch them. So . . . time to go up and get yourselves settled. Tomorrow will be kite-flying day, weather permitting."

And with Uncle Dangerfoot standing in the hallway, lightly tap-tap-tapping his cane on the floor, Norman and the hooligans followed Roxie up the stairs.

The boys went into the blue bedroom with the gray boats on the wallpaper, and the girls went into the yellow bedroom with the green willows on the walls. Sure enough, there were the lists of jobs the children had to do posted inside each door.

The girls poked their heads into the boys' bedroom: a set of bunk beds to the right and left. Norman had already put his backpack on a lower berth.

"What jobs do you have to do?" Roxie asked, and Norman read them off: "Freddy: Sweep porches, front and back; Norman: Mop kitchen

32

floor; Simon: Run vacuum over downstairs carpets."

"What did you get?" Simon asked the girls.

"Helvetia has to scrub the sinks in both bathrooms, I have to make all the beds, and Smoky Jo has to dust the furniture in the parlor," Roxie told him.

"Well, it could be worse," said Helvetia. "A lot easier than what we have to do at home."

Mrs. Tumbledry came up the back stairs just then and gave them each a washcloth and towel. "Time to do something quiet now, until bedtime," she said. "And don't forget to leave those dirty clothes outside your doors tonight."

Roxie looked the girls' room over. There were two double beds, a chair, and two dressers for clothes.

"I get a bed to myself!" Helvetia declared.

"That's fine," said Roxie. She didn't mind sharing a bed with Smoky Jo. The last thing in the world she wanted was to sleep with Helvetia Hagus. She opened her suitcase and began taking out the clothes her mother had packed, hanging them in the closet.

Helvetia and Smoky Jo had nothing but the clothes on their backs, and though Smoky Jo was glad to put her grimy things outside the door and pull on a nightgown she'd found in a drawer, Helvetia said she wasn't turning her clothes over to anybody. So she took off the T-shirt with the picture of a fist and the words SEZ WHO? on the front and the wet and sandy jeans, and dropped them on the floor beside her bed. Then she crawled under the sheets in a

34

T-shirt she'd found in one of the dressers.

Instantly, she gave a yell and threw off the covers, jumping out of bed faster than a top could spin.

"A crab!" Helvetia yelled. "Somebody put a dead crab in this bed!"

There was muffled laughter from across the hall.

"The boys!" screeched Smoky Jo.

"You wait till tomorrow!" Helvetia bellowed.

Mrs. Tumbledry tapped on the door and opened it. "Is everything all right in here?" she asked.

Helvetia held up the dead crab. Mrs. Tumbledry came inside and picked up a wastebasket. "Drop it in here," she said. "And remember, there's a baby sleeping in the room above." Then she took the dead crab with her as she left the room.

"Those boys are going to be sorry," Helvetia said, getting back in bed again.

"She always says that," said Smoky Jo. "And then they get even with her. And then"—she yawned—"there's nothing else to do."

"Well, there's plenty to do here," said Roxie. "Uncle Dangerfoot will see to that."

For a long time that night, Roxie lay awake, staring up into the darkness.

This was not quite the way she had imagined her vacation to be. It was always fun to have kids her own age to play with, but she might not have chosen the hooligans. And though Mrs. Tumbledry seemed nice enough, Roxie wasn't sure how she felt about the Widow.

36

Still, it was certainly a change from the little village of Chin-in-Hand, and Uncle Dangerfoot had been so kind to bring her along, a famous man like himself. He was always at work on some new project or invention. The cane that could change to an umbrella was one. The watch that could turn into a drinking cup was another. Sometimes he was simply writing a paper on some research project. But this time, because his work brought him to a beach, he'd said, he had decided to invite Roxie along—she deserved a treat.

"What will you be working on, Uncle Dangerfoot?" she had asked him in the car.

"Several new projects, my dear. I'm writing a paper on the types of grasses that can grow in sand and marshes," he had told her. "Not very exciting for you, I'm sure, but you and Norman will find plenty to do." Neither of them knowing, of course, that the hooligans would come too.

Scccccrape went a noise outside the window, and Roxie jumped. Her large ears picked up the slightest sounds, from the pounding surf way down on the beach, to the gentle closing of a cupboard door in the kitchen, to a baby's lullaby on the floor above.

She got out of bed and made her way to the window. But all she could see beyond it were the scraggly branches of a tree, their fingerlike twigs scraping against the house, and the pale moon shining through the clouds. And far beyond, the tall silhouette of another house looked forlorn and deserted against the sky.

Roxie knelt down, her arms resting on the

38

window ledge. Smoky Jo was a restless sleeper and had rolled and tossed so much that Roxie thought she must be terribly tired when she woke each morning. And Helvetia's snoring came in fits and starts. Roxie tried counting fireflies to see if that would make her sleepy, and then she counted stars. But it was hard to tell which ones she had counted after a cloud drifted by, and she had to start again.

All at once she jerked her head and stared hard at the house far down the beach. A light had come on in one of the windows. She was sure that Mrs. Tumbledry had told them that none of the other beach houses had been rented this summer. But someone must be there. And then the light went out, just like that. Well, Mrs. Tumbledry was probably wrong.

Roxie's knees were starting to hurt, and she was ready to get back in bed when, from . . . she wasn't sure where . . . she heard the murmur of men talking in low voices.

She held her breath, paying complete attention. Where could they be, and who would be prowling around? Robbers? She leaned forward until her head was almost out the window. All was black and all was quiet. Then . . . she thought she heard them again. But once more they stopped. And even though she didn't move an inch for the next five minutes, listening—both ears on alert, her eyes on the ground—the voices didn't come again and she didn't see a thing.

• FOOTPRINTS IN THE SAND •

When Roxie woke the next morning, she went to the window again, and this time she saw Mrs. Bitterworth walking along the garden path with a baby bundle in her arms.

Gray moss dangled from the tree branches, and an acre of willows and sea grass separated the house from the beach. It was a beautiful sight.

When Roxie turned away, she saw a different

sight, for Smoky Jo had fallen off the bed and lay curled up on the floor with her pillow, while Helvetia was sprawled on top of her blanket, one leg draped over the side of her mattress. Roxie dressed as quietly as she could, but suddenly a loud whistle split the air, followed by Uncle Dangerfoot calling the children to attention.

Helvetia opened one eye. "What is this, the navy?" she said. And then she opened both eyes. "Where are my clothes?" she yelled.

Indeed, the wet and sandy clothes she had dropped beside her bed were gone, as well as the shirts and pants that Roxie and Smoky Jo had put outside their door the night before. And far off in the kitchen, Roxie could hear the *chuga, chuga, chuga* of a washing machine.

Roxie pulled on some fresh things and went

out into the hall where Simon and Freddy were rubbing their eyes and peering over the railing at Roxie's uncle on the floor below.

"Good morning!" Uncle Dangerfoot called. "Kite-flying day! Come eat a hearty breakfast, and after you've done your chores, we'll head for the beach."

"What time does he get up, anyway?" asked Freddy.

"Early," Roxie said, and she couldn't help noticing that yesterday Freddy had been wearing a pair of tan shorts and a green T-shirt, and now he had on a pair of jeans that were so long they almost covered his feet, and an orange T-shirt with a cute panda on the front.

"It's all I could find!" Freddy snarled. "Laugh and you'll be sorry."

"Why? You'll put a crab in my bed too?" Roxie said.

"I didn't do that, Simon did," Freddy told her.

"Just what we wanted to know," Roxie said, and went back into the bedroom.

Helvetia was standing at one of the dressers. She was pulling open drawer after drawer, yanking out clothes and tossing them in the air. Stray shirts and pants and socks were flying overhead like sea gulls, half-covering Smoky Jo.

"Leave me alone! I need to sleep!" Smoky Jo whimpered.

"I'm afraid you'll have to get up," Roxie told her. "When my uncle blows his whistle, he means business."

Smoky Jo sleepily crawled to the window and looked out to make sure it was really morning.

Another batch of clothes flew through the air.

"I'm not wearing any of this!" Helvetia fumed.

"Got no choice," Smoky Jo told her, looking down toward the backyard. "Our clothes are hanging on a clothesline, dripping wet." And she too began picking up stray pieces of clothing to put on as the washing machine below chugged on with another load.

"This is the stupidest, dumbest place I've ever been!" Helvetia said, grabbing a pair of baggy pink shorts and a lavender shirt with a ruffle around the collar, the only things that were big enough to fit her. "And the first person to laugh at me gets it right in the mouth!"

Smoky Jo was having her own problems with a little dress that looked as though it had been

46

designed for a three-year-old. There were kittens all over the front and back.

"No wonder people leave this stuff behind," she muttered. "I can't wait till I get this one dirty."

Uncle Dangerfoot, neat and crisp in safari shorts and a sun helmet, stood at the doorway of the dining room, ushering the children in with a cheery smile. *Is this the same uncle who had growled at them yesterday?* Roxie wondered. Helvetia must have decided she'd still rather be here than back home in Chin-in-Hand, because she was pushing Smoky Jo toward the table, and she thumped Freddy on the head for grabbing a biscuit before he'd even taken his seat. Simon was already there, trying not to attract attention in a shirt with wide black and white stripes across it.

"What are you—a prisoner on a chain gang?" Helvetia guffawed.

"Look at yourself," Simon muttered. "You look like the frosting on a birthday cake."

"And how are all of you this morning?" Uncle Dangerfoot asked as he passed the sausage. "You slept well, I hope?"

"Like a log," said Norman.

"Not me," said Smoky Jo. "The only bed I've ever slept in is my crib. Too many kids in my family for us all to have a real bed. Can't ever remember waking up when I wasn't looking at the world through the bars."

Mrs. Tumbledry chuckled. "Then you ought to put on your happy face, child, because here you have regular-size beds and pillows, and all the breakfast you can eat."

48

And so the meal continued over scrambled eggs and oatmeal, and Uncle Dangerfoot's melodious voice telling about his latest jungle adventure with Lord Thistlebottom from London: ". . . and there we were, our vehicle stuck in a streambed, the water rising, and the savage rhino poised to attack if ever we opened a door. . . ."

Roxie looked about the table, unsure of whether the hooligans were listening at all, for the biscuits were disappearing almost as fast as Mrs. Tumbledry filled the basket.

But as soon as the table was cleared, each hooligan went about his or her assigned task, eager to be done with it and out of the house—a big house like this that needed a lot of cleaning. The kitchen alone was as large as some of the hooligans' cottages back home. As Uncle

Dangerfoot went about inspecting their work, Roxie told him, "Last night I saw a light in a window way down the beach."

Uncle Dangerfoot stopped and looked down at her. "And where were you?" he asked.

"At my window. I had trouble getting to sleep. It just came on and went right off again."

"Hmmm," said her uncle. "Perhaps Mrs. Tumbledry was mistaken, and another house was rented for the summer after all. Carry on, my dear."

It wasn't long before the children had finished their work, and Uncle Dangerfoot showed them a new way to the beach—along the willows, across a small bridge, through the sea grass, and over the dunes.

"I don't care about a stupid kite," Helvetia told

Roxie and Smoky Jo. "I want to look for something disgusting, even worse than a sand crab."

"To put in Simon's bed?" Roxie asked.

"To put on Simon's plate!" said Helvetia.

"I'd like to see him eat it before he even guessed what it was." Smoky Jo chortled. It was interesting to Roxie that the hooligans could be as mean to one another as they had once been to her.

It did seem to be taking the boys a long time to put their kites together, so the three girls headed barefoot down the beach toward the rocks that divided the Widow's property from the beach houses beyond. They passed a few dead fish and a clump of seaweed, a jellyfish that quivered there on the sand, and various shells with small creatures tucked up inside.

It was all disgusting stuff—Roxie had more fun picking up shells—but there was nothing Helvetia could use to trick Simon.

As they approached the huge rocks marking the north boundary, Roxie suddenly stopped. "Look!" she said, and pointed.

Helvetia shrugged. "What?"

"Those big footprints in the sand."

They were mysterious indeed, for they began at the large boulders, came forward about fifteen feet, then turned around, went back, and disappeared right into the rocks.

"A ghost who lives in the rocks," Smoky Jo said in a spooky voice.

"A ghost with big feet," said Roxie. "Size thirteens, at least. Wonder what he saw that scared him off."

"I don't care," said Helvetia, turning around. "All I want to do is find something nasty to put on Simon's plate. Maybe even something alive and crawly."

"Good thing Simon chose something that was dead. If that crab was alive it could have pinched you," said Roxie as she followed along beside her.

Helvetia only shrugged. "You know what else I think is dead?" she said. "That baby. Have you heard it cry yet?"

"Maybe Mrs. Bitterworth is just a good mother," said Smoky Jo. "She's always singing to it."

"Yeah, the same song, over and over, a million times," said Helvetia. "It's a recording, I'll bet."

There were a couple of kites in the air when the girls got back. Roxie could see them bobbing and tossing about, whichever way the breeze was blowing. They were awfully close together, though, and Roxie wondered why the boys didn't move farther apart and give each kite its own space in the sky.

Uncle Dangerfoot, however, was intent on examining a particular blade of sea grass with a magnifying glass, unaware of the battle going on up above.

Like ninja fighters, the kites got closer and closer, twisting and turning, almost colliding, then suddenly darting apart again, their tails whipping about behind them. Norman was in on the fun as the boys bumped into one another, trying to knock one of the other kites down.

And then Smoky Jo gave a screech that sounded like five rusty gates, all swinging at the same time. "Freddy's got my underpants tied to the tail of his kite!"

Sure enough, tied to the tail of one of the kites, along with the other rags and strips of paper, were a couple of socks from off the clothes-line and a pair of underpants with JOSEPHINE stenciled on the bottom.

And the next thing anyone knew, the wiry little girl with the screech-owl voice had tackled Freddy Finch, knocked him down on the sand, and was pounding him on the chest while all the kites crashed down on top of them.

·WHO'S *HE*?·

As Uncle Dangerfoot marched them back to Windswept House, he lectured the hooligans on the necessity of letting their words do their fighting for them.

"You," he said, pointing his cane at Freddie Filch, "had no right to take her clothing and fly it high in the air."

"And you," he said, as the cane changed

direction and settled on Smoky Jo, "should simply have asked Freddy to take it down!"

"Yeah, right," muttered Helvetia, "I'd like to know what old Dangerfoot would say if *his* knickers were flying overhead for everyone to see!"

All of them, however, were ordered to shake the sand from their clothes, hose off their legs, and quietly retire to their rooms until lunchtime.

Helvetia was out of sorts because she still had not found the right something to put on Simon's plate—something that could trick him into eating it. She lay on her bed staring at the ceiling, arms crossed over her chest.

Smoky Jo sat by the window, watching a flock of gulls swoop and congregate outside the back door, waiting for Mrs. Tumbledry to throw out the morning's bread crusts. All Smoky Jo could talk about was how to get even with Freddy.

Roxie was in the big chair in one corner, listening to all the noises the old house made no matter what time of day or night. Right now she could hear the clatter of dishes in the kitchen as Mrs. Tumbledry prepared lunch. There was the soft sound of the lullaby the Widow sang to her baby. But this time Roxie's marvelous ears picked up a new noise that she had not heard before—a more distant *clank* and *clunk*.

But Norman heard it too, for just then he appeared in the doorway.

"Where do you think it's coming from?" he asked. "That funny noise . . ."

"I think it's somewhere above us," Roxie said.

"I can barely hear it," said Helvetia. "Why do you care?"

Norman shrugged. "I don't know. If Uncle Dangerfoot is working in the library, and Mrs. Tumbledry is in the kitchen, and the Widow's with her baby, and all the rest of us are in our rooms, somebody else is in the house. . . ."

Clink . . . clunk . . . clunkity . . . Then silence again.

"I'll go see what my uncle thinks," said Roxie. But when she checked downstairs, the library was empty.

She went back up and found everyone in the boys' bedroom, Smoky Jo with a grin on her face and eyes wide.

"What's the matter?" Roxie asked. And then, looking around, "What's going on? What is that noise, and where's Freddy?"

"He went up the back staircase to find out," said Smoky Jo.

60

"What? He knows the third floor is off-limits!" Roxie exclaimed.

Smoky Jo's grin grew even wider. "Yeah. Maybe he'll be sent home."

It was the longest five minutes Roxie had spent in quite a while. Now the hooligans were really going too far. Helvetia worried too.

"We'll get busted for sure," she said. "We'll all get blamed."

"Dangerfoot is going to send us back faster'n you can blow your nose," said Simon.

After a bit, there was a creak of stairs, footsteps in the hallway, and Freddy burst into the bedroom, holding a paper bag.

"Freddy!" Roxie cried. "You know we're not supposed to . . ."

He opened the bag and held it out, and his

eyes had nothing but mischief in them. "Put your hand in there," he said.

Roxie looked at him and then at the bag. "Why? What is it?"

"Go ahead. Just put your hand in. It won't hurt you," said Freddy.

Roxie had the same feeling she'd had back on the island when all the hooligans were after her and she'd had to show them she was braver than she was. With all of them watching now, she gingerly put her hand inside the bag. Then she quickly pulled it out. *"What is it?"* she asked. "Is it alive?"

Freddy laughed, put his own hand in the bag, and pulled out a woman's wig.

Everyone stared.

"Where did you get that?" Helvetia asked.

62

"Just nosing about. Widow's in the nursery with the door closed, so I took a quick look around—her room, a couple empty bedrooms— and guess what? There's a small staircase that must lead to the roof. I think the noise is coming from up there."

"You went in her room?" Roxie cried. "Go put that back, Freddy! Quick! She might come out any minute!"

Freddy turned on his heels and disappeared down the hallway again.

The soft singing was still coming from above, but Roxie and Norman and the hooli- gans huddled down with hands over their ears. The lullaby stopped, and Roxie waited for a scream from the Widow, or a yell from Roxie's uncle.

But at last Freddy came through the door and then they could hear footsteps on the back staircase going down.

"Whew!" said Helvetia.

"Don't you ever do that again, Freddy." It was Simon giving the orders this time. "You could have got all of us in trouble. Especially nosing around in someone's personal stuff."

"I didn't take anything," said Freddy. "Just borrowed the wig to show you. Bet the Widow's as bald as a baseball."

"Well, it's not any business of yours if she is," said Roxie.

"So maybe it was your uncle up on the roof," Norman suggested.

Roxie thought about it. "The footsteps did sound a little heavy coming back down."

"And those little clinks and clunks have stopped," said Simon.

What took their place, however, was the shrill whistle once again as Uncle Dangerfoot called them to lunch.

They filed obediently down the stairs and took their seats at the table.

As the children ate their sandwiches and soup, Uncle Dangerfoot tweaked the ends of his mustache and announced that it might be nice if lunchtime was spent with each person telling of some new discovery he or she had made since coming to Windswept House. Any little everyday happening would do. He wanted them to see their surroundings as a scientist or detective might. For example, he told them, he had found a type of weed growing on the dunes that very morning that would ordinarily be found on far more southern shores.

"I found a dead fish with its eyes rotting out," said Simon.

"Ah, yes. To be expected, I suppose," said Roxie's uncle.

"I discovered that it takes a good fast run on the beach to get a kite up in the air," said Norman.

"Jolly good!" exclaimed Uncle Dangerfoot. "And to hold the string tight as you let it out."

Helvetia stuffed a last bite of baloney into her mouth, chewed awhile, and said, "I saw some footprints in the sand that started at the rocks and turned right back round again."

That had been Roxie's discovery, but she had

to listen as Uncle Dangerfoot seemed to find this the most interesting of all.

He stopped chewing, lifted his napkin from his lap, wiped his mouth, and set it down again. "And what did you conclude from this, Helvetia?"

"That they probably weren't ours, I suppose."

"A scientist cannot just suppose, my girl. A detective cannot just guess. If the footprints began at the rocks and ended at the rocks, what does this mean? That someone came from within the rocks?" Now Uncle Dangerfoot sounded like a teacher.

"Either that or somebody climbed up and over," Helvetia told him.

"And since none of you are allowed to go

beyond the rocks, what can you conclude?"

"That either somebody's going to get his butt smacked, or there's somebody else walking around out here," said Helvetia.

"Good girl! A detective you are not, but there's hope. As we are the only guests here along this section of beach, however . . ."

A good place to remind him of the light she had seen, Roxie thought.

"I saw a light in the house beyond the rocks," she told the others. "It was late last night."

Her uncle's back straightened as he studied his niece. This time he seemed to be taking her seriously. "Tell me more," he said.

"I was watching for fireflies from my window upstairs, and all at once I thought I saw a light down the beach. So I leaned out the window a little farther, and there was a light in an upstairs window of that house beyond the rocks. But it only lasted a couple of seconds and then it went out."

"If it had not been there before, and it was not there after, and you only saw it for a few seconds, what do you conclude?" asked her uncle.

Roxie wondered what kind of answer he wanted to hear. "That maybe I was dreaming and didn't see anything at all?" she guessed.

"Possibly, or . . . ?"

"That someone is there who doesn't want us to know about it?"

"By Jove, you've got it, my girl," he said. "But a hypothesis is still a hypothesis until it can be tested and proved. . . ."

"*What* hippopotamus?" asked Smoky Jo.

But Uncle Dangerfoot had already pulled a notebook out of his safari vest and was taking notes.

And that afternoon, as Roxie passed the door to the library, she was quite sure she heard him say to the Widow Bitterworth, "I think he's come. . . ."

• TROUBLE •

The next day, Uncle Dangerfoot took his crew to the beach for a swim. Windswept House provided bathing suits for its guests, so all the children wore blue bathing suits with white lettering on the front that said WINDSWEPT, INCORPORATED.

Roxie's uncle taught them to duck under the waves as the breakers rolled in toward shore.

Smoky Jo was so small and light that the ocean picked her up and tossed her about like a Frisbee, and Freddy complained of water up his nose. The hooligans liked trouble more than anything, but they were no match for the sea.

In the afternoon, Uncle Dangerfoot taught them the rules of badminton and croquet, but they were better at bopping one another over the head with their rackets, and whacking one another's croquet balls far out across the lawn. Smoky Jo finished last at croquet, and in typical Smoky Jo fashion, she pulled up all the stakes and wickets and flung them into the bushes, while the others were going inside. She always seemed to leave a reminder of where she had been.

That evening, as the children were washing

up for dinner, Helvetia showed Roxie a tiny dish of a white paste she was bringing to the table.

"Want a bite?" she offered.

Roxie studied the white stuff. "What is it? Mayonnaise?"

"Simon Sauce," Helvetia said, and then whispered in Roxie's ear, "Sea gull poop in mayo. For Freddy, too."

Roxie gasped. "Helvetia, no! You can't!"

"Says who?" Helvetia demanded, and marched on into the dining room.

And as if that wasn't bad enough, when Roxie got to the table, there was the Widow Bitterworth, and she had brought her baby along, wrapped in its blue-and-yellow blanket and tucked into a small baby basket, which the Widow carefully

74

set on the floor beneath the table when the meal began.

Everyone seemed to be on their best behavior with the Widow present, and Helvetia would not, could not, dared not bring out that horrid little dish during mealtime, Roxie thought.

From the head of the table, Uncle Dangerfoot smiled at the assembled guests.

"We are pleased that the Widow Bitterworth could join us this evening, as we are all enjoying our stay in her wonderful house," he said. "So I asked Mrs. Tumbledry to prepare her favorite dish, which happens to be salmon with hollandaise sauce, and potatoes and peas . . ."

"Yuk," Roxie heard Simon mutter. "I'll take mayonnaise with mine!" She was probably the only one at the table who heard Helvetia's little chuckle in the seat next to her, and noticed the wink that passed between the largest girl at the table and the smallest.

As the meal began, Uncle Dangerfoot said, "All of us, I'm sure, are enjoying our stay in this huge, delightful old house."

He lifted his glass. "Indeed we all do! To Mrs. Bitterworth and her wonderful house, and to Mrs. Tumbledry, our cook!" Mrs. Tumbledry poked her head in from the kitchen and blushed.

"Anyone want some mayonnaise?" Helvetia asked, holding her little dish out toward Simon.

"I'll take some," said Norman, extending his hand.

In that instant, Roxie rose from her seat, as though reaching for the bread basket, and knocked the dish from Helvetia's grasp onto the floor.

"Oops! Excuse me!" Roxie said as Helvetia glared at her, eyes wide with surprise.

"Roxie, are those the kind of manners we use at this table?" Uncle Dangerfoot scolded.

"No, sir," said Roxie from the floor, where she was quickly scooping the sea gull poop off the rug. But she had done it and she was glad! She glanced around at all the feet under the table. Uncle Dangerfoot's polished boots, the hooligans' scruffy sneakers, and there, right across from her, the Widow Bitterworth's big foot resting smack-dab on top of the baby in the basket, as though to keep it from getting away.

* * *

Helvetia was still furious with Roxie that evening, but Roxie didn't care.

"Who knew that Norman was going to reach for it?" she said.

"Well, he just got in the way," said Helvetia. "Wasn't my fault." She yanked her nightshirt on over her head, jerked back her blanket, lay down, and turned her face to the wall.

Smoky Jo decided to sleep on the floor. "I fell

out of that bed three times last night!" she complained. Still, she flopped about and bumped the bed and moaned in her sleep, keeping Roxie awake. So once again, Roxie got up and sat by the window, watching for that light to come on again in the house beyond the rocks. Uncle Dangerfoot had definitely seemed interested when she'd told him about it.

But this time there was no light, and she wished Smoky Jo would quit her moaning and tossing so that she could get some sleep. Roxie wondered what it might have been like if the hooligans hadn't come. Some of the time they were fun to be around, and some of the time they reminded her of all the days they had been mean to her and Norman, and tormented them at school.

And now, because of her big ears, it seemed like sounds were tormenting her. She could hear not only the waves breaking out on the shore, but Helvetia's throaty snores, Smoky Jo's constant rustlings, the tree frog calls—who knew such tiny frogs could be so loud!—and a moth fluttering against the raised window.

And then, just as she was beginning to feel sleepy, her ears picked up the sound of men's low voices, just like the night before. This time the voices seemed to be somewhere below her window.

Roxie jumped to her feet. Were they outside the house? On the porch? Should she wake Mrs. Tumbledry?

She tiptoed across the room and softly

80

opened the door. She could hear the men a little better, so they must be in the house. But who were they? Robbers?

"What's the matter?" Helvetia whispered sleepily.

"I hear something," Roxie said.

"What?"

"I don't know. It sounds like men talking. But Uncle Dangerfoot's the only man in this house. I think we should wake Mrs. Tumbledry."

"I thought that was only for emergencies," said Helvetia. "Where's the emergency? Let's you and me go find out."

"Hey! What's going on?" squeaked Smoky Jo from the floor.

"There are men talking somewhere close by,

and we're going to find out who they are," Roxie whispered. "Come on, if you want, but you can't make a sound."

"They won't even know I'm there," Smoky Jo promised, and scrambled off her pillow. The girls went out into the hall, but at the first creak of the stairs, the boys' bedroom door opened.

"What's going on?" whispered Norman.

"I hear men talking," Roxie whispered back. "We're going to check."

"Then we should all go," Norman said. "Let me wake Simon."

And when Simon had joined them, they heard a voice say, "Don't go without me."

Freddy came running out into the hall in his underpants, then ducked back into the room for his trousers. Roxie put one finger to her lips and

82

the hooligans stood stock-still, listening.

"I think I hear them now too," whispered Simon. "But if they're robbers, we ought to be armed."

"I'll get a baseball bat," said Norman, going back into the bedroom. He came out carrying the bat and a wooden clothes hanger, which he handed to Simon. Freddy got a Ping-Pong paddle.

Helvetia armed herself with a candlestick from a table in the hallway, Roxie got a butterfly net, and Smoky Jo brought up the rear, holding a can of bug spray.

Quiet as crabs, they made their way down the dark staircase in the moonlight.

• THE BABY •

Sure enough, there were men's voices coming
from the library at the end of the hall, the one
room in the house without windows. Up close,
Roxie could now tell that one of the voices was
her uncle's.

Her heart pounded as she imagined what
might be going on inside. Perhaps her uncle was
tied to a chair. Perhaps one of the men had a gun!

There seemed to be a heated argument going on, even though the men were keeping their voices low.

"I tell you, I'm going to try it," said one man in a low growl.

"Is that a robber?" whispered Freddy.

"Shhhh," said Norman.

Then Uncle Dangerfoot's frantic voice: "I won't allow it! Someone might get hurt!"

"I'll bet he's talking about us!" whispered Roxie.

The hooligans crowded closer, clutching their weapons, each of them wanting to hear what was going on, and in the pileup, Freddy tumbled against the door and knocked it wide open.

There sat Uncle Dangerfoot in his bathrobe, one bare foot on top of the wastebasket, and

86

sitting across from him was Mrs. Bitterworth, without her wig, smoking a fat cigar.

Roxie stared.

"Lord Thistlebottom!" she cried, recognizing the man who had piloted the helicopter that had rescued her and the hooligans from the island a few months before.

"By Jove, now we've done it!" said Lord Thistlebottom, snuffing out his cigar. And then, finding himself surrounded on all sides by armed hooligans in their nightclothes, he slowly shook his head and motioned for them to have a seat.

Uncle Dangerfoot gave a weary sigh. "Close the door, Roxie," he said. "We'll at least try not to waken Mrs. Tumbledry. I see that we have no choice but to let you in on a secret of great importance. I can only trust that none of you will

tell a soul what I am about to share with you."

Roxie frowned. Her parents had taught her never, ever, to keep a secret that ought to be shared with her parents.

"I can't keep a secret from my mom and dad," she told him.

"Right you are! Of course! We will share it with your parents, too," her uncle said. "You all know, I'm sure, about Lord Thistlebottom's famous book, *Pitfalls and How to Survive Them*. Right now, we are working on a marvelous invention, so secret we can only refer to it as the 'baby.'"

"Is that what you carry around in a bundle and put to bed at night?" asked Helvetia.

"Right again!" said Lord Thistlebottom. "But I fear that our nemesis . . ."

"Your what?" asked Freddy.

"Our . . . enemy, I guess you'd call him. No, our competitor—one Alfred Applejack the Third—has possibly followed your uncle here, knowing how closely we work together in our travels. That cunning, crafty, scurrilous fellow has tried to beat us to any invention we've ever worked on, wanting to claim it as his own. I may be wrong; he might this very moment be sitting at a pub in Boston without the slightest idea that I'm here. Or, he might be somewhere close by, using every excuse known to mankind to discover the idea we're working on—an invention which, if successful, will shape the future of any man, woman, or child who might find himself or herself in a perilous situation, desperately in need of an extraneous device of such . . ."

"Speak English, Lord Thistlebottom, will you?" said Helvetia.

"We can't tell you any more at this time," said Uncle Dangerfoot. "We're not even sure it will work. We came all the way here to this isolated beach for a test run, but there are still some mechanical problems—"

"But then, I don't understand why you wanted to bring me here," Roxie interrupted. "It's a wonderful place for a vacation, but . . ."

"I'm afraid I kept the secret from even your parents, my dear girl," her uncle said. "But once we'd rented this house, far away from prying eyes, with Lord Thistlebottom disguised as a woman and our invention wrapped up like a baby, we thought it would be even more convincing that we were simply here for a seaside

vacation if we had a child about. And I immediately thought of inviting my favorite little
niece. And when these hooligans . . . I mean . . .
your friends showed up unannounced, Lord
Thistlebottom and I quickly realized this would
make it all the more believable. Even dear Mrs.
Tumbledry fell for it. We hoped that if Alfred
Applejack were indeed to follow us here, he
might fall for it too."

"Fall for what, exactly?" asked Helvetia.

"That this is merely a happy holiday for a
niece and her chums," said Lord Thistlebottom.
"A summer camp, even, and a poor widow woman
renting out rooms and taking her babe for walks
in the garden. Hopefully, if the conniving Alfred
Applejack does show up around here, he will
quickly assess the situation, decide he is wasting

his time, pack up his bags, and go home."

"So you don't really want to play ball with us on the beach, Uncle Dangerfoot?" Roxie asked. "It's all just an act?"

"It might sound that way, my dear, but, no! It has awakened the child in me—that long-ago lad who played kick-the-can after dark—and suddenly I have a whole list of things I want to do yet that I think you'll enjoy," Uncle Dangerfoot said. "But, of course, part of the time I must withdraw to this library to work out the finishing touches on our design."

"Or up on the roof clinking and clunking about?" asked Norman, looking hard at Roxie's uncle through his thick glasses.

"You knew about that?" Lord Thistlebottom asked, surprised.

"Roxie's ears can pick up anything!" Helvetia said proudly.

Uncle Dangerfoot looked around the room at the six children. "If you think you can't keep our secret for the rest of the week we're here, we will call off the test run, pack up tomorrow, and take you back to Chin-in-Hand. It's up to you entirely."

For a moment no one answered. Then Simon said, "I vote we stay."

Simon and Helvetia and Freddy and Smoky Jo all put their hands together, one on top of the other, to show they meant it. Roxie and Norman joined in. "Stay and keep the secret," they said.

"As long as Thistlebottom and Unc are honest with us," added Helvetia, and Roxie and Norman agreed.

"And what's this all about?" asked a voice, for the door to the library had opened, and there stood Mrs. Tumbledry in her nightgown, her robe pulled about her shoulders. Staring at Lord Thistlebottom in the long brown dress, but without the wig and veil, she said, "Who's he?"

Uncle Dangerfoot had to explain all over again, apologizing for having misled her.

"You mean, she's a he?" the housekeeper asked.

"Quite so, to all appearances," Lord Thistle-bottom explained, "but I will be glad to get out of this dress when the week is over. And I will be especially glad to be rid of that scratchy wig and veil."

"Well, butter my biscuits!" Mrs. Tumbledry

96

declared. "I never in this world know what to expect when I take on a new job."

"And now to bed, everybody!" Uncle Dangerfoot declared, clapping his hands together. "This is quite enough excitement for one night."

As the children were going back upstairs, Freddy said, "I sure would like to know what they're working on up on the roof."

Roxie turned on him. "No, you wouldn't, Freddy. You're not even going to think about going up there!"

"No harm in thinking, Roxie," said Simon.

Even Norman agreed. "No harm in imagining."

"What if he dreams about it? Is that against the law?" asked Smoky Jo.

Roxie wasn't sure how she felt about anything as she crawled back into bed. She had always trusted her uncle before, and she didn't like to feel that she and her friends were simply part of a secret plot. Still, it all seemed quite harmless, even if old Applejack did show up.

And yes, she too was curious about what her uncle and Lord Thistlebottom were building up on the roof; it would serve them right if the children took a peek, after trying to trick them for two days. With that decided, she closed her eyes and slept soundly the whole night.

But when she woke up the next morning, something was terribly wrong.

Smoky Jo . . . was missing.

• SUPERDISAMBIGUATION •

"Where's Smoky Jo?" Roxie asked, nudging Helvetia awake.

Helvetia slowly sat up and stretched. "Search me," she said, yawning.

Smoky Jo had been the last one up the morning before—the one complaining that they were wakened too soon—so it seemed strange to find her gone.

Roxie poked her head out the door, but the second-floor hallway was empty, and when Helvetia went to check the bathroom, she came back to report that Smoky Jo wasn't there, either.

Just as they were putting on their shoes, however, the small, wiry girl ambled into their bedroom, a wide smile on her face. "That was the best sleep I've had since we got here!" she declared.

"Where were you?" Roxie and Helvetia said together.

"I went up to the third floor and crawled into that crib, that's what I did," Smoky Jo told them.

"You slept with the 'baby'?" Roxie exclaimed.

"Yep. That 'baby' is as big as a watermelon, all wrapped up in blankets. I just borrowed one of those blankets, wrapped myself up tight,

100

and slept in that crib all the way through till morning."

"What if old Thistlebritches had found you?" Helvetia asked, clearly worried that the hooligans might be sent home before the week was up. "What if he notices that someone was in there?"

"He won't. I put the blanket back on the 'baby' and got out of there just in time," Smoky Jo assured them. "She's one heavy kid, let me tell you. Maybe I'll peek inside all those blankets some morning and see what kind of invention it is."

Roxie shuddered. Trying to stop the hooligans was like trying to tame a cyclone, and this was sure to end badly, she was certain.

The children had the breakfast table to themselves that morning, as both men were working up on the roof. Every now and then there was a distant clink or a muffled clatter.

"Can't they be seen on the roof?" Roxie wondered aloud.

"Not easily," Norman said. "There's a balcony on the back of the house with a wall around it. I went out this morning with binoculars and looked up."

"Old Six-Eyes-Norman," Simon taunted. "Two on your head, two on your glasses, and two on the binoculars. If you ever lost your glasses, you couldn't go anywhere, could you?"

The hooligans were starting to sound like they had back on the playground of Public School Number Thirty-Seven, Roxie thought. Now she was definitely beginning to feel sorry they had come along.

Perhaps Uncle Dangerfoot sensed this too when he came down for his own breakfast, because when he had finished, he declared that this would be another day at the beach—starting with a race. After chores were done, the children would compete to see who could run the fastest from the rocky boundary on the north to the inlet on the south. Mrs. Tumbledry would pack a picnic lunch, and afterward they would have the afternoon to swim and wear themselves out.

Roxie's uncle was more enthused about the idea than any of the children, but nonetheless, the children changed into bathing suits and helped carry the blankets and buckets and shovels and spades and Frisbees down to the water. The three shortest children—Freddy, Roxie, and Smoky Jo—lined up at the rocks to race when Uncle

Dangerfoot gave the signal. He held a small red flag in one hand, his watch in the other.

"Go!" he said, dropping the flag, and the kids were off, not quite like a shot, but Smoky Jo was in the lead from the very beginning. She passed the sand dunes and Windswept House, and reached the inlet before either Roxie or Freddy. Freddy gave up before he even got there.

"Who cares?" he said, panting as he came back to where the others were waiting, and flopped down on the blanket Mrs. Tumbledry had brought.

The tallest children were a bit more excited when they lined up and started the race. Helvetia was ahead at the beginning, but she began to slow, and Simon reached the inlet first. Norman came in last.

"Hey, Norman!" Freddy jeered. "You're the caboose!"

"The six-eyed caboose," said Helvetia.

"Do we get a prize?" Simon asked.

"It's not whether you win or lose that's important, my boy, it's how you run the race," said Uncle Dangerfoot.

"Well, that stinks!" said Simon, but Mrs. Tumbledry brought out the lemonade, which was met with loud hoorays, and Uncle Dangerfoot went back to the house to work some more on his invention.

While the children were eating an early picnic lunch, a breeze came up that cooled their faces and fanned their hair, and it wasn't long before the gentle Mrs. Tumbledry was nodding off.

"What'll we do?" Helvetia said. "I'm bored."

"Let's dig a hole and put somebody in it," said Simon.

"Me!" said Freddy. "Put me in it and see if I can dig myself out."

And suddenly everyone was digging away with shovels and spades and buckets and bare hands, sand flying every which way. Mrs. Tumbledry snored on.

Deeper and deeper went the hole. Every so often Freddy would climb down inside it, and Helvetia would say, "It's got to be deeper, way over his head." Then they'd pull Freddy out and they all would dig some more.

Water seeped into the bottom of the hole, and the sand grew heavy and damp. More water and more water still, and finally Smoky Jo peered over the side and said, "That's deep enough. Let's put him in it."

So they lowered Freddy down into the hole. When he stood upright, the water came to his ankles, the opening of the hole was two feet above his head, and Freddy was grinning.

Everyone sat back and took a breath.

"You ready, Freddy?" Helvetia called. "Somebody time him to see how long it takes him to climb out."

Norman checked his watch.

"Ready, set, go!" Simon said, and Freddy set to work, busily clawing at the sides of the hole to make handholds.

But suddenly Roxie and the hooligans realized that the more he dug, the faster the sand began

to cave in around him. First just a little, then a little more.

"Hey!" yelled Freddy.

"It's caving in!" screamed Roxie, as the sand piled up around Freddy's knees. Mrs. Tumbledry startled awake, and hearing the children scream, she screamed too.

The next thing Roxie knew, Uncle Dangerfoot was bounding up over the rim of a sand dune and across the beach. He yanked off his jungle helmet, gave it three shakes, and a rope ladder flopped out from around the brim.

Uncle Dangerfoot lay down at the edge of the sand, and holding tight to the top of the ladder, he dropped the rest into the hole.

"Climb, Freddy. Try to pull your feet out and climb," he called.

"Oh, that pitiful boy!" cried Mrs. Tumbledry, wringing her hands.

The sand was pouring in faster still, but somehow Freddy managed to pull out one foot, swing it onto a rung . . . then the other foot. With Roxie's uncle and Simon and Helvetia and Mrs. Tumbledry all helping to hold the top of the ladder, and Roxie and Norman and Smoky Jo all holding back sand at the top, Freddy managed to get himself, rung by rung, up the rope ladder and onto the beach above.

Everyone collapsed on the sand, panting, after the rescue, and the children needed no scolding, having been frightened far too much already. Mrs. Tumbledry could not believe that she had fallen asleep and allowed this to happen.

"It will be a lesson to us all, Mrs. Tumbledry,"

Uncle Dangerfoot said as he led the children back to the house for showers. But Roxie heard him murmur under his breath, "That hole would have been the perfect place for a Blasto-Sonic-Liftomatic. Absolutely perfect!"

There was chicken and dumplings for dinner that night. It smelled so delicious that Lord Thistlebottom, as Widow Bitterworth, decided to come down and eat with the others. He would continue wearing the dress and veil and wig as long as the experiment lasted, just in case there were prying eyes about, he said.

The hooligans, hungry, were still not being as polite as they should. They were not used to passing platters around the table and waiting patiently until the food got to them.

"Watch that you don't take all the dump-lings!" Simon said as Helvetia piled her plate.

"Quit hogging the butter, Smoky Jo!" Helvetia said in turn.

But when Freddy said, "C'mon! Pass the bread, Four-Eyes," to Norman, Lord Thistlebottom suddenly rose from his chair and leaned forward over the chicken, staring hard down the table.

Every hooligan froze in his seat. Every hand paused in midair. Every mouth stopped chewing. Lord Thistlebottom leaned farther and farther until the front of his brown dress was almost in the gravy. And then he lifted his veil with one gloved hand and looked directly into Norman's eyes.

Why Norman? Roxie wondered. *What did he do?*

112

"Norman," Lord Thistlebottom said, "take off your glasses."

Terrified, Norman slowly reached up and pulled them off.

Lord Thistlebottom studied him some more.

"Tell me," he said. "Do you use a flashlight when you need to post a letter after dark?"

"No . . . ," said Norman, his lips scarcely moving. "I never even post letters after dark."

"Do you turn on the lamp when you get up for a drink of water in the night?"

Norman shook his head.

"Can you tell who is ringing your doorbell after dark without turning on the porch light?"

"Yes," said Norman.

"Aha!" said Lord Thistlebottom, and he pulled a small magnifying glass from the pocket of his brown dress. He left his chair and came around to examine Norman's eyes. "By Jove, I think what we have here is a rare gene, passed down from Queen Victoria herself. Tell me, Norman, did any of your ancestors come from England?"

"Uh . . . my great-grandma did," Norman said, trying not to blink in the distinguished man's face.

114

"Just as I thought. I am looking into the eyes of a person with a vestigial tapetum lucidum, giving him superdisambiguation," Lord Thistlebottom announced with satisfaction. And then, straightening up, he looked about the table and said to the others, "This fellow has the superb ability to see in the dark far better than the rest of us."

"Why didn't you just say that in the first place?" asked Smoky Jo, but no one heard except Roxie.

"What an honor!" Lord Thistlebottom said, sitting down again and dropping the veil.

"Indeed!" said Uncle Dangerfoot. "Norman, we are proud to have you at our table."

Norman began to smile, wider and wider, as the hooligans gaped at him with awe. And for

115

the rest of the meal, they passed the platters to Norman first before they took anything more themselves.

It was that very evening, when everyone was settling down for the night, that another pair of eyes made an appearance. The children had shaken the sand out of their shoes and were preparing to go upstairs. Roxie followed her uncle from room to room, turning off lights and closing curtains. She had just reached up to pull the cord on the living room drapes when she screamed, for she found herself staring directly into the face of a strange man right outside the window.

· ON THE ROOF ·

"A man!" Roxie cried. "He was standing right there, outside the window."

Others came running, but even in the dress and veil, Lord Thistlebottom got there first.

"Did he have a short mustache?" he asked Roxie, his voice urgent.

"Yes," Roxie said.

"Did he have a thin nose?"

"Yes," Roxie said.

"Did he have black hair that rose up in a point above his forehead?"

"Exactly!" said Roxie.

"I knew it! Alfred Applejack the Third has been snooping around, so he must have got wind that your uncle was about."

"Then we have to work all the harder to convince him that I am here as an uncle on vacation with my niece," said Uncle Dangerfoot.

"But what about you?" Helvetia asked Lord Thistlebottom. "I'll bet old Applejack would believe I'm here for camp before he'd believe there's a woman in that getup of yours."

"I have never been out of my room without my wig and my dress. Except, of course, when I was in the library, where there are no windows for Peeping Alfreds," Lord Thistlebottom answered.

At that moment, Norman and Simon came running in, panting hard.

"Where have you been?" Uncle Dangerfoot asked. "I thought everyone was inside."

"We ran out and chased him, sir!" Norman said, trying to catch his breath.

"Right out to the road!" said Simon, giving Lord Thistlebottom a short salute. "Then we lost him, but we gave that weasel a good run."

"Well done! Well done!" said Uncle Dangerfoot.

"Alfred may be a cheat and a thief, but he's clever," Lord Thistlebottom told them. "To bed, everyone! We will need all our wits about us to keep one step ahead of Alfred Applejack. Make certain all curtains are closed, and I shall double-lock the doors."

The boys were still talking about it as they went upstairs. They'd never had the chance to chase a spy back in Chin-in-Hand, and perhaps they'd never felt so important or needed.

Roxie woke to tinkering sounds before breakfast again. Smoky Jo had barely climbed out of the crib on the third floor and slipped down the back stairway, she told them, before Lord Thistlebottom had come into the room to unwrap the "baby" and take it up the narrow stairway to the roof balcony.

Smoky Jo snuggled up with her pillow on the floor and slept a bit longer, but Roxie's ears

120

picked up all the peculiar noises coming from above. She could hear the *clink* and *clonk* of metal parts being bolted in place, the *tink* and *tonk* of screws dropping onto the balcony floor, and the *sprink* and *spronk* of springs being tested, as well as the occasional cries from Lord Thistlebottom and Uncle Dangerfoot: "To the left, I tell you!" "By Jove, I think we've got it!" and "Oops! Not again!"

After the children were wakened and had their breakfast, and once all chores were finished, Mrs. Tumbledry organized a game of volleyball on the lawn. Roxie could not help glancing up at the roof every so often, but the high wall around the balcony hid the grand invention from view.

When the two men came down for lunch, however, Roxie could tell by the look on her uncle's face and the tone of Lord Thistlebottom's voice that the project had not been going as well as they'd hoped. As soon as lunch was over, they retired to the library with their papers and drawings and mechanical instruments to go over their design once again.

Helvetia, to Roxie's surprise, told Mrs. Tumbledry to take a rest, that they would clear the table and clean up the kitchen, and the kind housekeeper was glad to do it. Besides teaching the children to play volleyball, she had baked two pies for dinner and put a meatloaf in the oven.

"I guess I do need a lie-down," she agreed. "I'm so tired, I'm about as useful as a cat in a canoe." And in she went to the parlor, took off her shoes, and stretched out on the sofa.

While they washed and dried the last of the plates, Helvetia whispered, "As soon as we're finished here, let's sneak up to the roof. I want to see what it's like up there."

Roxie couldn't see much harm in that. Smoky Jo and Freddy had already been up on the third floor, and all they wanted was a peek at the balcony. So to the sounds of Uncle Dangerfoot and Lord Thistlebottom's arguing in the library, and Mrs. Tumbledry's soft snoring in the parlor, Freddy led the way up the back staircase to the third floor, then on up a narrow staircase to a trapdoor at the top. They pushed it open and climbed out onto the walled balcony and softly closed the trapdoor behind them. Clouds swirled overhead.

There, on the floor, was a strange contraption

that looked like a harness or vest, with a football player's shoulder pads, a wrestler's belt, and a motorcyclist's helmet. The leather shirtfront was covered by a metal panel with all sorts of buttons on it. Various wires stuck out here and there, with a little hook in back.

It was quite intriguing, and when Helvetia picked it up, she saw that it was flexible, and could . . . possibly . . . be folded down to the size of a watermelon.

Of course she had to try it on.

"Put your arms straight up," Simon said, helping out. Norman adjusted the shoulder pads.

"Now turn around so we can fasten the back," Freddy instructed.

"And adjust the belt," said Smoky Jo, as Roxie handed Helvetia the helmet.

"What's the hook for?" asked Norman.

"Who knows?" said Helvetia, "but I've got enough on me as it is."

She looked very strange in the weird contraption. There were small missile-shaped objects on the back of the belt, battery cases on either side, and a start/stop switch in front.

"It's heavy!" said Helvetia, her knees bending a little under the weight.

"I wish I had a camera," Freddy said with a laugh. "Helvetia the Horrible!"

"We should smuggle it out some night and give it a try," Simon suggested.

"I think we should try it right now," said Smoky Jo, and before anyone could stop her, she reached out and flipped the start switch just as the trapdoor opened behind them.

126

"Stop!" shouted Uncle Dangerfoot, clamboring onto the balcony, Lord Thistlebottom right behind him. But it was too late.

There was a buzz, a whir, a squeak, a hiss, and suddenly Helvetia rose straight up in the air.

• THE BLASTO-SONIC-
LIFTOMATIC •

"Helvetia!" all the hooligans yelled at once.

Roxie could only stare as the soles of Helvetia's shoes hovered ten feet over their heads.

"Come down, child!" begged Uncle Dangerfoot.

"By Jove, it works!" exclaimed Lord Thistle-bottom, just as Mrs. Tumbledry opened the trap-door to see what all the commotion was about.

"What's she doing?" Mrs. Tumbledry cried, crawling onto the balcony. She stood up and whacked Lord Thistlebottom on the shoulder. "You're no lady, sir! Who cares about your inven-tion with that child bobbing around up there in fear for her life?"

But Helvetia wasn't bobbing about for long—she hovered only a few seconds more, and then, like a Fourth-of-July rocket, she suddenly turned face down and shot this way and that in

a zigzaggy line, a fizzing sound coming from
the little rockets on her belt. She zoomed past
them one last time, then buzzed to the beach,
skimming the tops of the sand dunes. Finally,
she started to slow, and then . . . *whop!* Down
she went.

"The emergency parachute!" Uncle Dangerfoot cried. "They didn't hook on the parachute!"

Everyone rushed back down the winding
staircase to the third floor, then down two more
flights, along the hallway, and out the back
door. They reached the shore just as Helvetia
was digging her way out of the sand.

"My precious child!" cried Mrs. Tumbledry,
hurrying over.

"It's a wonder you didn't break every bone in
your body!" Uncle Dangerfoot exclaimed, lifting

off the helmet. "Does anything hurt?"

"No, but I was slapping at every button in sight, and none of them worked. Your stop switch wouldn't stop it, and your emergency button isn't worth a dead fly," Helvetia said.

"That's because you didn't attach the parachute, my girl!" said Uncle Dangerfoot, taking Helvetia's arm and helping her up. "That's what the hook was for, and here's the parachute. It was lying right there on the balcony floor." He waved what looked like a neatly folded tablecloth. Of course the hooligans had ignored it completely.

"But we've almost got it working!" Lord Thistlebottom said excitedly. He carefully removed the heavy harness off Helvetia's back, and tucked it under the hem of his long brown dress to hide it. "Let's get it in the house before

Alfred Applejack sets eyes on our invention."

Once inside the library, the children were in for a scolding. Lord Thistlebottom set the apparatus on the table, and Mrs. Tumbledry inspected Helvetia for bumps and bruises. Only a scraped knee, a bump on the elbow, and a small hole in the T-shirt with a fist on the front.

"You—all of you—have seriously disobeyed us," Uncle Dangerfoot began. "You had no permission to go up to the third floor, no permission to go to the roof, and certainly no permission to put on our invention." And looking straight at Helvetia, he said, "You could have been killed."

"Not to mention possibly wrecking the Blasto-Sonic-Liftomatic," put in Lord Thistlebottom, carefully inspecting the leather vest and control panel for damage.

"So that's what you call it!" said Simon.

"Well, let me tell you, the buttons and switches could stand a little work," said Helvetia, rubbing her knee, but she couldn't hold back a grin. "Wildest ride I ever had in my life."

But Mrs. Tumbledry crossed her arms over her chest. "What's the good of it, I ask you?" she said, glaring at the men. "A harness that pops up in the air is about as useful as a back pocket on a shirt. That apparatus is dumb as dirt, if you want my opinion. And here I thought I'd been hired to cook and clean for an ordinary family for a week."

"Why, Mrs. Tumbledry, the Blasto-Sonic-Liftomatic can take a person places," Uncle Dangerfoot said.

"A person has to go up in the air to get from here to a sand dune?" The housekeeper

134

humphed. "That's like going around your elbow to get to your thumb."

"If our invention had been on the market, and Freddy Filch here had been wearing one yesterday at the beach, he could have shot himself right up out of that hole in the sand and been free as a frog in a matter of seconds," Roxie's uncle said.

Lord Thistlebottom pulled off his veil, then his wig, and fanned himself with a sheaf of papers. His brown dress was beginning to look splotched and worn, and one of the seams at the sleeve was pulling out. Then he began:

"Please take a chair, Mrs. Tumbledry. And sit down, all of you. You are aware, are you not, that Daniel Dangerfoot and I have traversed the globe . . ."

". . . traveled around the world, as it were," Uncle Dangerfoot put in.

". . . and have encountered many a terrifying situation," Lord Thistlebottom continued. "It was in the heart of Africa that we were charged by a raging bull elephant. . . ."

"In the Australian outback, we were knocked to the ground by a berserk kangaroo. . . ." said Uncle Dangerfoot.

"Poachers had us cornered in the Congo, crocodiles overturned our canoe in the Amazon, and a tiger could have killed us both in India," said Lord Thistlebottom. "Only by extreme diligence and quick thinking did we find our way out of each situation, but were we wearing a Blasto-Sonic-Liftomatic . . ."

136

". . . we could have flipped a switch and shot straight up in the air, out of harm's way, and steered ourselves to safety," finished Uncle Dangerfoot.

"Sure, if the stupid thing had worked," said Helvetia. "But don't feel bad. You could always charge admission and give kids a wild ride."

"My dear, we do not invent things for amusement, but for scientific advancement," Lord Thistlebottom said. "Angry as I am that you disobeyed us, I must thank you for giving our invention a trial run. And though it still needs a bit of work, I am convinced that once we have a patent on it, explorers will thank us, and it will be known all over the world as the Thistlebottom-Dangerfoot Blasto-Sonic-Liftomatic."

137

"Uh . . . the Dangerfoot-Thistlebottom Blasto-Sonic-Liftomatic, I believe," said Uncle Dangerfoot.

"We'll save that debate for another day," said Lord Thistlebottom breezily. "For now, let us put our invention to bed, and after dinner we'll take a fresh look at the blueprint." He put on his wig, then his veil, for when they left the four walls of the library, who knew if Alfred might be looking in?

"Let's bundle it up well," Uncle Dangerfoot said. "Alfred Applejack will try anything to get his hands on this, and should he slip into our house sometime in the night, he will be looking for an invention, not a baby."

Mrs. Tumbledry shook her head as she watched the two men go upstairs. "Bundle the two of *them* up and sail 'em out to sea, if you ask me," she said. "You'd think that piece of junk was a flesh-and-blood baby. Well, I've got my meatloaf to check. If you children think you can stay out of trouble till dinnertime, I'll tend to my cooking." And she headed for the kitchen.

Roxie and Norman and the hooligans stretched out in the parlor.

"Wow, Helvetia, that was some ride!" said Simon. "Wish it had been me!"

"What was it like?" asked Freddy.

"Like riding a rocket," Helvetia said. "Something started hissing and spitting, and I was pressing first one button, then another to get it down, when it suddenly turned me sideways and started zigzagging every which way."

"It might be useful, though, to get yourself out of a dangerous fix if you traveled the world

139

like Thistlebottom," Norman said wistfully. "But sort of heavy to carry around as you trekked through a jungle."

The children thought about that awhile.

"But once the kinks are sorted out, I can see how somebody else might like to get his hands on it and claim he invented it himself," said Roxie.

"Yeah," Norman agreed. "Your uncle and Lord Thistlebottom have been working on it a long time. It would be a shame if someone stole their idea."

"I wouldn't worry about Alfred Applejack getting it," said Simon importantly. "There's only one of him, and"—he did a mental head count—"there are nine of us."

But the following morning, there were only eight.

• ALFRED •

Their excitement over the Blasto-Sonic-
Liftomatic kept them up till late, and the following morning, the children began straggling
down to breakfast one or two at a time.

"Let the others sleep!" Uncle Dangerfoot
said. "Since this is a vacation, not a camp, I
guess there's no reason we must all rise with the
roosters." He was mellow sounding indeed.

But just as Mrs. Tumbledry set down bowls of fresh berries, Lord Thistlebottom entered the dining room. He looked very grave indeed. He was still wearing the long brown dress, but not the wig nor the veil, and he held a small piece of paper in one hand.

The children looked up, surprised.

"Attention," he said, and every child put down his or her spoon. Every face turned in his direction. Mrs. Tumbledry paused in the kitchen doorway with a plate of muffins, and Uncle Dangerfoot lowered his cup of coffee.

"It seems that despite our security measures, Alfred Applejack invaded this house during the night and left me this note. I just discovered it."

"What?" cried Uncle Dangerfoot, leaping up,

142

but Lord Thistlebottom held the paper out in front of him and began to read:

> To whom it may concern, and you know who you are: Since you have refused to let me in on your past inventions, I want to inform you that your new apparatus is now in my possession. I saw the inglorious lift-off yesterday, and I intend to get a patent on this and claim it as my own. Unless, of course, you help me get it working properly, and then the three of us could enjoy the fortune we would make together. If you refuse, you may never see your so-called "baby" again.
>
> Alfred Applejack III
>
> PS You can ditch the dress, Lord T. I'd know you anywhere.

Uncle Dangerfoot's face was as white as the cream for his coffee. "Where did you find the note?" he asked.

"In the crib, where we put our invention last night," Lord Thistlebottom told him.

"That dastardly, deplorable, diabolical, deceitful deadbeat!" cried Uncle Dangerfoot, pounding the table.

"But the strange thing is," Lord Thistlebottom continued, "our invention is still there."

"What?" everyone cried.

"I read the note, then unwrapped the blankets, and there she was—the shoulder pads, the harness, the belt, the rockets—everything folded up nice and tidy, just as it was before."

"How strange!" said Mrs. Tumbledry. But then, because the invention was safe, she said,

144

"Here are some muffins, children, to go with your porridge. But save one for Smoky Jo, whenever that child decides to come down to breakfast."

Roxie and Helvetia exchanged horrified glances. Then Roxie turned to Lord Thistlebottom, her eyes wide. "Was . . . was anyone else in the crib?" she asked.

"In the crib? Of course not. Who would be sleeping with our invention?" he asked.

In answer, Roxie and Helvetia scooted away from the table and went dashing upstairs. They checked their bedroom, the bathroom, then the apartment up on the third floor. All they found was one of Smoky Jo's little socks under the crib, and, terrified, they took it down to the table.

Roxie faced her uncle and Lord Thistlebottom.

"I think Alfred Applejack took the wrong bundle," she said, and quickly explained how Smoky Jo had been sneaking upstairs after everyone else was asleep and climbing into the crib beside the invention. "It was the only way she could get a good night's rest," she told them. "In the mornings, she would come back down before anyone discovered her there. And she always rolled herself up tight in a blanket, just like the Widow Bitterworth's 'baby.'"

"Well, my mercy! This means the poor child has been kidnapped!" cried Mrs. Tumbledry.

"Let's go for the sheriff," Uncle Dangerfoot said at once.

"Good luck with that!" said Mrs. Tumbledry. "Sheriff Gunshot takes August off and goes fishing."

146

"That's incredible! What do people do for protection when he's not here?" sputtered Lord Thistlebottom.

"Well, in August, people pretty much take the law into their own hands, best they can. But generally it's a slow month for crime here in Buzzard's Roost," Mrs. Tumbledry said. "Oh, the poor child! What if he hurts her?"

"I wouldn't worry too much about that," Uncle Dangerfoot told her. "He's not a man to do physical harm, and it's not the first time old Applejack's kidnapped someone for ransom. A few years back he kidnapped a grandmother, and he treated her so well—tea every afternoon—that she didn't want to leave when the police showed up, and she refused to press charges. Just the same, we will go rescue Smoky Jo ourselves, as soon as we figure out where he has taken her. First, we'll search this property for clues." He took the pink sock from Roxie and held it up. "Clue number one," he said. "Place all found clues on the table in the library."

Roxie and Norman and the hooligans all started talking at once about how Alfred Applejack must have climbed up the tree during the night, crept in through the third floor window, lifted a blanketed bundle up out of the crib, and lowered it into his bag before leaving the note and climbing out the same way he'd climbed in. Smoky Jo had said that she'd never slept better in that crib, so she probably slept through it all.

"I'd sure like to have seen old Applejack's face when he opened that sack and unwrapped the bundle," Freddy Filch said, a grin crossing his face. And the others started to grin as well.

"I'd like to have seen Smoky Jo's face when she woke up and saw him!" said Helvetia as they left the room to start the search. "Can't you just hear the screech she made when she realized she'd been kidnapped?"

"He must've thought he'd kidnapped a wild-cat," said Simon. "Nobody messes with Smoky Jo when she's mad."

"But where do you figure he's taken her?" asked Roxie. "The note didn't even say how Lord Thistlebottom was supposed to get in touch with Alfred."

"That means they can't be far off," said Norman. "There will probably be another note in a day or two."

"Do you think they could be in that beach

house beyond the rocks?" Roxie asked her uncle as everyone scattered to find their shoes and prepare for the search.

"It's the first place I thought of," Uncle Dangerfoot answered. "But we need to be clever about it. You and Norman will come along with me."

So Uncle Dangerfoot and Roxie and Norman searched north; Lord Thistlebottom took Freddy and Simon and searched south; and Mrs. Tumbledry and Helvetia walked out to the road, looking for clues.

Roxie's eyes carefully searched the sand dunes and sea grass as they walked. The roar of the ocean was so loud that it almost drowned out a distant barking of dogs that she had not heard before when she had explored the beach with the other girls. Fortunately, her wonderfully large ears picked up everything.

"Can you hear all that barking, Uncle Dangerfoot?" she asked.

Her uncle stopped and listened. "No, not yet," he said.

Norman didn't hear it either. But as they got closer and closer to the house beyond the rocks, the barking grew louder.

"That's Hailstone House, Mrs. Tumbledry calls it," Uncle Dangerfoot said. "She thought no one had rented it this summer."

"The one with the high wall around it?" said Norman. "I'd bark too if I could never see over the top. What's the good of living by the ocean if you can't see it?"

Uncle Dangerfoot helped them crawl over the

huge rocks at the north border of the property, and when they finally reached the gray-shingled house, they saw that there were no trees in the yard, and the shutters on one of the top windows were closed. The dogs, however, barked ferociously, and began leaping up against the wall, their claws scratching and clawing as they growled.

"We'll go around to the gate and call out!" exclaimed Uncle Dangerfoot. "After all, a child has been kidnapped! We must use all possible means to rescue her."

"If she's here," said Norman.

"Right," said Uncle Dangerfoot. Then he called out, "Hello? Is anyone at home?"

The dogs, of course, all Dobermans, reached the gate first, and they leaped high up against its

152

iron bars, saliva dripping from their mouths, in a frenzy of barking.

"Hellllo!" Uncle Dangerfoot called again, in his mightiest voice. "Is anyone here?"

But again, only the sound of the sea and the barking.

"We'd better head back," he said. "If Smoky Jo is in that house, it would be better if we came at night, when the dogs are sleeping. And so far, we have no clue that she's there."

But Roxie wasn't so sure. She lingered a moment after Uncle Dangerfoot and Norman started back, then turned and caught up with them, ears to the wind.

When they all gathered in the library an hour later to discuss what they had found, Roxie told the others that Smoky Jo might possibly be in the shingled house beyond the sea grass, because the shutters on one of the windows were closed, while the others were wide open.

"We think that Alfred Applejack came in a car and took her off to the village somewhere, because of fresh tire tracks out on the road," Helvetia told them.

"Well, we think she's been carried off in a rowboat, because there were footprints leading down to the inlet," said Simon.

So that afternoon, everyone traded places. Those who had looked for clues at the inlet went to the rocks instead. Those who had discovered tire tracks went to the inlet. Roxie and Norman went out to the road, but the tire tracks they found there could have belonged to anyone.

All they saw were the flocks of buzzards trading places in the row of dead trees that disappeared over the rise of the hill.

They met again for tea in the library, then switched search places once again, and gathered a third time to share what they'd learned. Nothing anyone had found was very helpful—a bottle cap, a flip-flop, and the wrapper from a toffee candy. Nothing that had belonged to Smoky Jo that anyone could remember.

"Well, all I can say is old Thistlebritches better find her," said Helvetia, as Roxie and Norman and the hooligans circled the house one last time before dark, worn out and not a bit wiser. Everyone was almost too tired to eat. Roxie's uncle and Lord Thistlebottom sat in the library debating what to do next.

Just before bedtime, it was Roxie who found the second note, slipped under the front door:

Okay, so I picked up the wrong bundle. If you want to see this precious girl again, place your invention on the porch by midnight, and I will leave the girl there in its place.

A. A.

Helvetia left a note of her own on the porch for Alfred Applejack:

Go eat your socks.

156

• THE DEAD OF NIGHT •

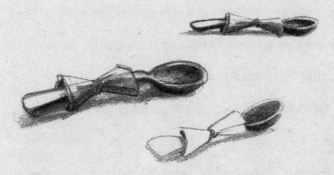

When they showed the note to Uncle Dangerfoot and Lord Thistlebottom, however, Roxie's uncle said, "Perhaps it's time to make a deal. No invention, even one we've been working on for two years, is worth the life of a child."

Lord Thistlebottom nodded. "He's a rascal, though. We could give him the invention and he could still ask for ransom. He could make us sign a statement that says he was the one who invented it in the first place, not us."

"Children, leave this to us. It's time for you to get some sleep. We'll need you to be fresh and wide awake tomorrow, for it could be another trying day," said Uncle Dangerfoot.

All the children went upstairs and got into bed, but once the others were asleep, Roxie and Norman crept back down, crawled out a downstairs window, and headed for the rocks and the tall, shingled house with the wall around it beyond. Roxie knew she should have told her uncle where they were going, but she was certain he would have insisted on going with them. And two children creeping along over the sand were not nearly as visible as two children with a man over six feet tall.

"I thought I heard sounds that could have been voices when we were there this morning," Roxie told her friend. "But they just weren't clear or loud enough for me to be sure."

"Well, I sure didn't hear any," said Norman. "How could your ears pick up voices when all I could hear were the waves breaking on shore and all those dogs barking?"

"Elephant ears," Roxie said, grinning. "How can you tell where we're going when I can't even see my feet in the dark?"

"Eagle eyes," said Norman.

They had no flashlight, but Norman's night vision warned them of every rock, every log, anything they might possibly trip over there in the sand. It was a little more difficult climbing over the huge rocks between them and the neighboring beach house, but they remembered the route Uncle Dangerfoot had chosen, and made it to the other side.

As they drew closer to the gray-shingled house, their feet made no noise at all. The dogs must have been asleep, for the children heard no bark, no growl. There was no sound from inside the house either.

When they reached the wall surrounding it, Norman's sharp eyes caught sight of something glinting in the moonlight. He crept over and picked it up.

"What is it?" Roxie whispered.

"A . . . a spoon," Norman answered, looking at it closely. "A spoon with a piece of paper wrapped around it, and a rubber band around that."

160

He unfastened the rubber band and, thanks to his superdisambiguation, he was able to read it to Roxie:

If anybody finds this, I'm a prisoner in the house with a jerk named Alfred. He doesn't hurt me, but his cooking is terrible. I poured his oatmeal down the toilet and stopped it up. Don't give him your invention, Uncle Dangerfoot. Get me out if you can, but his dogs will tear you to pieces.

Smoky Jo

"She is there! I did hear her voice this morning!" Roxie whispered. "What do we do now?"

But Norman was pointing straight up at the gray-shingled house; the shutters on the top

162

window were open this time. Roxie could just make out someone small holding something white. A flag, perhaps? A flag of surrender, meaning give Alfred Applejack whatever he wanted?

And then Roxie realized it wasn't a flag at all; it was a pillow. And the somebody—who had to be Smoky Jo—wasn't waving it, she was shaking it. Soon hundreds of white feathers were silently sailing out on the breeze, this way and that, filling the night air and drifting slowly down to the ground.

Roxie clapped one hand over her mouth to keep from shouting out Smoky Jo's name. When the pillow was emptied, Smoky Jo reappeared with a second pillow and shook that one out as well. Roxie and Norman waved their arms wildly to get her attention, but she obviously hadn't

seen them, for she disappeared from the window and didn't come back. They didn't dare make a sound for fear they'd wake the dogs.

They looked at each other and couldn't help smiling. Wait until Alfred Applejack found feathers all over the yard the next morning. You always knew when Smoky Jo had been around, because she was going to create as much trouble as she could as long as she was there.

"Did we just see that happen?" whispered Norman.

Roxie giggled. "Let's go tell my uncle we've found her!" she said.

It was close to midnight when they got back to Windswept House, and they crawled in through the window and tapped on the library door. Uncle Dangerfoot opened it at once; he and Lord Thistlebottom had not gone to bed at all.

"What is it?" he asked anxiously. "Not another child missing?"

"We've found Smoky Jo!" Roxie said excitedly.

"Where?" cried both men together.

Norman handed them the note, and Roxie explained how she thought she might have heard Smoky Jo's voice when they'd been there earlier, but hadn't been sure. Uncle Dangerfoot was so happy to know Smoky Jo was found that he forgot to scold Roxie and Norman for going out alone at night.

"Now, however," he told them, "it's time for you to spend the rest of this night in your beds."

"Yes! Excellent work!" Lord Thistlebottom

said. "So far it appears that Smoky Jo is not in any danger with Alfred, as I would have expected— he's clever as a fox and harmless as a rabbit. But from what you tell us, I can't say that he's not in any danger with her."

And that appeared to be correct, for the next morning there was another note slipped under the door of Windswept House:

Let me share in just 20% of your invention, and you may have this cantankerous, contentious creature back.

Alfred Applejack III

Lord Thistlebottom announced at breakfast that he and Uncle Dangerfoot had been up all night in the library working on the design of their invention. They were quite sure, now, that they had discovered the problem.

"What was the problem?" asked Norman.

"The distrometer that attaches the splort to the gizmus has to be shortened to increase the degree of tilt in the angulum," said Uncle Dangerfoot. "We'll fix it this very morning. . . ."

How could her uncle be concerned about his old invention with Smoky Jo still held captive? Roxie wondered.

". . . And we shall now use our marvelous invention to rescue that dear child. I should tell you that we had chosen the balcony to work on our secret project, because we wanted to keep it far from prying eyes. . . ."

"But obviously," put in Lord Thistlebottom, "we would have farther to fall if it failed. . . ."

"So obviously," Uncle Dangerfoot continued, "it should never be attempted without the parachute properly attached." And so, he told the children, one of the men would strap on the Blasto-Sonic-Liftomatic and go rescue Smoky Jo by hovering outside her window. If Alfred Applejack were the only person at the house other than Smoky Jo, the two men could have simply walked down the beach and forced their way in to rescue her. But even two men plus Mrs. Tumbledry and five rambunctious children were no match for a pack of ferocious, snarling dogs.

So once again the invention was hauled up onto the balcony, to be prepared for the grand lift-off when every screw was in place, every bolt tightened, every cable connected.

Meanwhile, Roxie and Norman and the hooligans made their own plan for how to distract the dogs while the rescue was taking place.

They busied themselves blowing up the rest of the balloons they had found when they'd first arrived and fastening them in tight knots with rubber bands. With waterproof ink, they carefully printed a message to Alfred Applejack on each one: things like "bug off," "game's over," "give up," and "sez who?" There were soon fifteen plump balloons ready for action, and the children stuffed them into five large pillowcases and placed them by the front door.

Finally Uncle Dangerfoot and Lord Thistlebottom came downstairs.

"At last we have something good to report," said Lord Thistlebottom, his shirt sleeves rolled up to the elbows and smudges on his face. "We have finally corrected the navigation problems with our Blasto-Sonic-Liftomatic. One of us— Daniel or I—will now attempt the rescue of that precious child." Nodding to Uncle Dangerfoot, he added, "Since both of us would like to be its pilot for this public preview, we'll toss a coin." He reached into his pocket and pulled out a quarter, handing it to Freddy.

"Wow, thanks," said Freddy, making to slip it into his own pocket, but Lord Thistlebottom stopped him.

"Flip it," he said. "What do you call, Daniel?"

"I call heads," said Roxie's uncle.

Freddy flipped the coin, and everyone stepped forward to see.

"Tails," Helvetia announced.

"Then tails it is," said Lord Thistlebottom. "To the roof, everyone! Let Alfred Applejack behold, in awe and envy, our magnificent creation!"

• A LIKELY TALE •

On the balcony, as the others stood along the wall waiting for the grand lift-off, Lord Thistlebottom fastened the cuffs of his shirt and straightened his collar. Then he held his arms up in the air as Uncle Dangerfoot hoisted the heavy contraption over his shoulders and buckled it up. He fastened the vest and the wide belt with the many instruments and buttons on it and adjusted the small rockets on the back. Both men made sure that the parachute was in place.

Then Uncle Dangerfoot stood ready with his list, and when Lord Thistlebottom gave him a nod, he began: "Stabilizer?"

"Check," answered Lord Thistlebottom.

"Windshaft regulator?"

"Check."

"Roter rooter?"

"Check."

"Booster beanie?"

"Check."

"Thruster buster?"

"Yeah, he's got it," said Helvetia. "Let's get this show on the road."

"You are cleared for takeoff," Uncle Danger-foot announced, adding, "Keep back, everyone."

174

Lord Thistlebottom took a deep breath and flipped the start switch on his belt.

There was a hiss, a ding, a creak, a ping, and suddenly, with a loud whoosh, Lord Thistlebottom—in his pin-striped pants and his white shirt with the silk cravat at the throat—began to rise into the air.

The whooshing sound grew louder the higher he went, his legs dangling beneath him, one hand grasping the harness, the other the belt. When he was fifteen feet above them, he tilted horizontally, flying around and around in a wide circle. All the children clapped.

Uncle Dangerfoot shielded his eyes from the sun, watching carefully. "Stabilizer!" he yelled, as Lord Thistlebottom suddenly dived and flew by.

The circling stopped, only to be replaced by a loop-the-loop!

"Equalizer!" commanded Uncle Dangerfoot.

While Lord Thistlebottom was practicing his circles and dives, Roxie and Norman and the hooligans scrambled back downstairs, grabbed their pillowcases full of balloons, and raced down to the beach. Over the rocks they went, and ran some more until they reached the high wall around the house where Smoky Jo was being held prisoner.

Simon, with his long legs and arms, managed to hoist himself up first, and soon all the children were seated in a row along the top of the wall, Uncle Dangerfoot not far behind. And circling above the sand dunes against a sunny sky was

176

Lord Thistlebottom, practicing maneuvers. The ferocious dogs in the yard were barking madly, leaping up against the wall, trying to reach the children's feet.

A man came running out of the house to see what all the ruckus was about. He had a short mustache, a thin nose, and black hair that rose in a point above his forehead, and he carried a croquet mallet in one hand.

He waved his arms and shook the mallet at Roxie and Norman and the hooligans, but they all began to chant: "Smo-ky Jo! Smo-ky Jo! Smo-ky Jo!"

There was an enormous crash, and the legs of a chair poked out through the shutters of the highest window in the house. Then the shutters themselves gave way, the chair fell to the ground, and Smoky Jo leaned out and waved to her friends.

"Smo-ky Jo! Smo-ky Jo!" the children continued to chant, and one at a time, they began releasing their balloons, sending them zooming, zigzagging this way and that, hissing and humming over the heads of the hysterical dogs. The dogs were so busy barking and howling and trying to bite the balloons that they did not immediately see the strange thing coming toward them in the sky, circling the house.

First it did a loop-the-loop.

Then it did a spin.

Then it did a corkscrew.

It began to descend and passed the chimney.

Then it passed the roof.

"Right over here!" Smoky Jo called, reaching up one hand toward Lord Thistlebottom in his magnificent machine.

But then the Blasto-Sonic-Liftomatic began to shudder and shake. It began to tip and jerk. Slowly it began to lose altitude, did a somersault right there in front of the children, and came down on top of Alfred Applejack III, while the terrified dogs went yipping and yelping to hide under the porch, tails between their legs.

The children leaped down into the yard, Uncle Dangerfoot after them. While her uncle hurried to help Lord Thistlebottom and check on Alfred, Roxie led her friends up the steps, into the house, and up the stairs to the top floor, calling Smoky Jo's name until they heard her answer, and they unlatched the door.

* * *

It was a grand parade back along the beach to Windswept House, Smoky Jo on Uncle Dangerfoot's shoulders. As for the Blasto-Sonic-Liftomatic, Norman carried the helmet, Roxie carried the belt, Helvetia carried the vest with the control panel, Simon carried one shoulder pad, and Freddy carried the other.

"It's all fixable!" Uncle Dangerfoot assured them.

Lord Thistlebottom had suffered no more than a bruise on his chin, and they left Alfred Applejack III sitting in the yard with the high wall around it, the dogs licking his face.

"Well, at least somebody loves him!" Smoky Jo said.

"He got a few bruises, that's all," said Uncle

Dangerfoot. "No point in taking him to jail, because it's closed, and the sheriff's not in town to arrest him."

They reached the beach house and carried the parts of the Blasto-Sonic-Liftomatic inside. The tired children sprawled out on the rug in the parlor, eating the cookies and drinking the lemonade that Mrs. Tumbledry had prepared for them.

"How did you know I was up there?" Smoky Jo asked. "He only let me open my shutters at night, and I couldn't turn on my lamp."

"We saw someone scattering feathers, and we figured it was you," Roxie told her.

"And I found the spoon with your message," said Norman.

"You leave a trail wherever you go, Smoky Jo," said Simon.

182

"Well, I know I'm going to give up sleeping in cribs," said Smoky Jo. "But I sure did love scattering all those feathers. That and stopping up his toilet. You should have seen the flood!"

"Hailstone House will never be the same," Mrs. Tumbledry declared. "I'm thinking that Mr. Applejack is going to get a hefty bill for damages to the room he locked you in."

"When you get your machine working again, Uncle Dangerfoot, do you think I could have a ride?" Smoky Jo asked Roxie's uncle.

"Haven't you had enough excitement for a while, my girl?" he answered. "No, I'm afraid our marvelous invention is intended for the jungle traveler, the mountain climber, the desert nomad, the Alaskan hunter, for it can do almost anything you want it to. . . ."

183

"Except land," murmured Simon.

"I'm sorry we have to go home tomorrow," said Helvetia, in as soft a voice as Roxie had ever heard. "And . . . I'm sorry about your invention, Uncle Dangerfoot."

"Sorry?" said Lord Thistlebottom. "Why, we consider it a success. Didn't you see me zooming around above your heads? Didn't you see me zigging and zagging and dipping and diving?"

"Yeah, especially diving. It's good at that," said Simon.

But Uncle Dangerfoot was excited as well. "We proved that it can rise, it can turn, it can pivot, it can tilt, it can do everything . . ."

". . . but land," said Freddy, trying not to laugh.

The two men, however, seemed as excited

184

as ever about the future of their invention—and when Mrs. Tumbledry begged them to tell her all about the rescue, they were glad to oblige:

"Oh, it was harrowing, let me tell you," Lord Thistlebottom began, one hand to his chest. "There I was . . . hovering above the roof tops . . ."

". . . in a machine yet to be perfected for the journey . . . ," put in Uncle Dangerfoot.

"Below me, the cold, bitter eyes of a desperate enemy, weapon in hand . . . ," Lord Thistlebottom said.

". . . and the gaping jaws of wild beasts, ready to tear him limb from limb . . . ," said Uncle Dangerfoot.

Helvetia and Simon and Norman and Freddy and Smoky Jo and Roxie lay with their hands behind their heads, listening to the tale and grinning at one another. Roxie knew that the story would take many a twist and turn each time it was told, and—just like the Blasto-Sonic-Liftomatic—it still needed a lot of work.

But suddenly Uncle Dangerfoot stopped in midsentence and said, "By Jove, I've got it! Just what we need for publicity! Let's make a banner to stretch across my trailer, proclaiming a fantastic new invention, and by the time we reach Chin-in-Hand, every person we pass will have heard of the Dangerfoot-Thistlebottom Blasto-Sonic-Liftomatic."

"The Thistlebottom-Dangerfoot Blasto-Sonic-Liftomatic," Lord Thistlebottom corrected.

"I'm not riding back home in that trailer again," Helvetia said, sounding more like herself.

"Right you are," said Uncle Dangerfoot. "I will turn in the car and trailer here and rent a minibus instead."

"A bus with a banner on the side about our new invention," said Lord Thistlebottom.

"How about a double-decker bus with all the kids riding on top?" asked Smoky Jo.

"Yay!" the other children cried.

"Capital idea! Jolly good!" cried Lord Thistlebottom. "Just the thing! A double-decker minibus with a Blasto-Sonic-Liftomatic banner in red and blue all along one side!"

And that's the way that Roxie and Norman and the hooligans returned home to Chin-in-Hand.

Also by
PHYLLIS REYNOLDS NAYLOR

The Alice Books

Starting with Alice

Alice in Blunderland

Lovingly Alice

The Agony of Alice

Alice in Rapture, Sort Of

Reluctantly Alice

All But Alice

Alice in April

Alice In-Between

Alice the Brave

Alice in Lace

Outrageously Alice

Achingly Alice

Alice on the Outside

The Grooming of Alice

Alice Alone

Simply Alice

Patiently Alice

Including Alice

Alice on Her Way

Alice in the Know

Dangerously Alice

Almost Alice

Intensely Alice

Alice in Charge

Incredibly Alice

Alice on Board

Now, I'll Tell You Everything

Alice Collections

I Like Him, He Likes Her

It's Not Like I Planned It This Way

Please Don't Be True

You and Me and the Space In Between

Shiloh Books

Shiloh

Shiloh Season

Saving Shiloh

A Shiloh Christmas

The Bernie Magruder Books

Bernie Magruder and the Case
of the Big Stink

Bernie Magruder and the
Disappearing Bodies

Bernie Magruder and the
Haunted Hotel

Bernie Magruder and the
Drive-thru Funeral Parlor

Bernie Magruder and the Bus
Station Blowup

Bernie Magruder and the
Pirate's Treasure

Bernie Magruder and the
Parachute Peril

Bernie Magruder and the Bats
in the Belfry

The Cat Pack Books

The Grand Escape

The Healing of Texas Jake

Carlotta's Kittens

Polo's Mother

The York Trilogy

Shadows on the Wall

Faces in the Water

Footprints at the Window

The Witch Books

Witch's Sister

Witch Water

The Witch Herself

The Witch's Eye

Witch Weed

The Witch Returns

Picture Books

The Boy with the Helium Head

Ducks Disappearing

I Can't Take You Anywhere

Keeping a Christmas Secret

King of the Playground

Old Sadie and the Christmas
Bear

Please DO Feed the Bears

Sweet Strawberries

Books for Middle Readers

All Because I'm Older

Beetles, Lightly Toasted

Being Danny's Dog

Danny's Desert Rats

Eddie, Incorporated

The Fear Place

How I Came to Be a Writer

How Lazy Can You Get?

Josie's Troubles

Maudie in the Middle

Night Cry

One of the Third-Grade
Thonkers

Roxie and the Hooligans

The Solomon System

Zack and the Turkey Attack

Books for Older Readers

Blizzard's Wake

Cricket Man

The Dark of the Tunnel

Ice

Jade Green

The Keeper

Sang Spell

Send No Blessings

A String of Chances

Walker's Crossing

Walking Through the Dark

The Year of the Gopher

Looking for another great book?
Find it
IN THE MIDDLE.

Fun, fantastic books for kids
in the in-be**TWEEN** age.

IntheMiddleBooks.com